Second Teeline Workbook

REVISED EDITION

I.C. Hill and Meriel Bowers

Heinemann Educational Books

London

Heinemann Educational Books Ltd
22 Bedford Square, London WC1B 3HH

LONDON   EDINBURGH   MELBOURNE   AUCKLAND
HONG KONG   SINGAPORE   KUALA LUMPUR   NEW DELHI
IBADAN   NAIROBI   JOHANNESBURG
PORTSMOUTH (NH)   KINGSTON

British Library Cataloguing in Publication Data

Hill, I. C.
   Second Teeline Workbook — Rev. ed.
   1. Shorthand — Teeline — Problems, exercises etc.
   I. Title   II. Bowers, Meriel
   653′.428   Z56.2.T4

   ISBN 0-435-45346-7

Printed in Great Britain by Richard Clay (The Chaucer Press) Ltd,
Bungay, Suffolk

Contents

Preface

This book is intended for use by those who have already mastered
Teeline theory, either from *Teeline: Revised Edition* and its com-
panion, *First Teeline Workbook: Revised Edition*, or from *Teeline
Shorthand Made Simple*.

The Second Teeline Workbook: Revised Edition includes
suggestions and guidelines for the development of speed and
extension of vocabulary. Students who understand the principles
outlined should then be able to adapt them to fit their own
particular needs.

All the outlines given have been tested for safety and legibility
at speed, but they do not necessarily constitute the *only* acceptable
outline in any specific case.

For ease of dictating, the passages have been divided into 10-word
lines, thus facilitating reading at any speed. The numbers in
brackets at the end of each exercise refer to the total number of
words.

It cannot be too strongly stressed that the contents of this book
are suggestions only, and that they may be adopted or rejected as
the individual wishes. Nevertheless, it is our hope that they will
prove to be useful for reference purposes and in the acquisition of
the higher speeds.

I. C. Hill and M. Bowers
September 1983

How To Make the Best Use of This Book

1 Study each unit and practise the outlines given before attempting the exercises. Using these outlines, the word groupings list at the end of the book and, if necessary, *Teeline Word List*, put the passages into Teeline.

2 Read back from your Teeline notes, preferably to your teacher or to someone who can check the accuracy of your reading from the book.

3 Now practise the passage by reading it through to yourself until you can read it from your Teeline notes at a normal speaking speed, at the same time tracing over the outlines as you read. This helps to link the writing movement with the thought or spoken words.

4 Pick out and practise separately any outlines which cause hesitation in reading or which seem difficult to write.

5 *Only now* are you ready to try the passage from dictation. Try it first at a speed within your capability. If you find yourself unable to get down every word, get down as many as you can. You may have to leave a gap here and there, but you should not give up half-way. It is important that you train yourself not to stop until the piece is finished.

6 Read it back, checking it from the book if necessary and fill in any gaps which you had to leave. Always check each 'take' in this way before going on to another attempt. Take particular notice of those words you had to miss.

7 Now try the passage again; at the same speed if you did not manage to take it all down, or at a higher speed if you did.

8 When practising word groupings, do not try to memorize the shape of the outline as this is not necessary, but think instead of the sounds represented, for example, 'able-ob' – 'able to obtain', 'above-tioned' – 'above mentioned', 'Act-Parl' – 'Act of Parliament', etc. This will help you to recognize the outline when transcribing your notes, even if it is not as well written as it should be.

Remember :
Reading back is as important as taking down.
Accuracy is as important as speed. Aim first for 100 per cent accuracy – speed will come with practice. If you cannot read back your notes, the whole point of taking down the passage is lost.

When you have achieved your target speed on short passages, try longer ones to build stamina. Stamina needs to be built up as well as speed and accuracy.

1 Improving Your Notes

Many of the following words are frequently mistranscribed. They need to be practised so that the precise differences in the shapes and sizes of the outlines can be maintained, regardless of the speed at which they are being written.

.... in .... an .... on .... any

.... you .... we .... your .... our

[............ yet

.... if .... for

.... while .... where

.... this .... these .... those

.... as .... is .... has .... his

.... us .... so

.... can .... could

.... shall .... should

.... will .... would

.... far .... from

.... on .... with .... the

.... January .... June

.... her .... high

.... small .... smaller .... similar

.... appeals .... appears

...... ✗ ... affected ...... ✗ .... effected

.... open .... upon

Exercises

1 It is quite likely that the representative has already left   *(10)*
the office as his car is no longer in its   *(20)*
normal parking space.   *(23)*

2 I shall be delighted to help with the external painting   *(10)*
if you should wish it, but so much will depend   *(20)*
on how much time will be allowed.   *(27)*

3 People who own home freezers are unable to make as   *(10)*
much use of them as they would like when prices   *(20)*
of fruit and vegetables remain high because of adverse weather   *(30)*
conditions.   *(31)*

4 January and June are two quite contrasting months. During
[January   *(10)*
we attempt to brighten up those dark winter days by   *(20)*
planning what we shall do in June and the other   *(30)*
summer months.   *(32)*

5 Bond paper is good quality paper and has a watermark   *(10)*
which indicates the name of the manufacturer. When this is   *(20)*
read from left to right one knows that one is   *(30)*
using the correct side of the paper. Corrections are more   *(40)*
easily made on this side because it has a more   *(50)*
even texture.   *(52)*

6 Why is it that if we are late leaving home   *(10)*
for the office in the morning everything that can possibly   *(20)*
go wrong will do so? Why are the traffic lights   *(30)*
always at red? What is it that makes us choose   *(40)*
the wrong driving lane so that the lights change again   *(50)*
and yet again as we sit waiting impatiently to move   *(60)*
off? It would appear that some jinx has fallen upon   *(70)*
us which is almost certain to last for the whole   *(80)*
of the day.   *(83)*

2

7 Dear Mrs Small,
    Thank you for your letter dated 2nd   (10)
February concerning our Express Coach service to
                                     [Manchester.
    I was   (20)
sorry to note that the revised arrangements at Manchester
                                       [are (30)
not as convenient for you, but the terminus was changed   (40)
following requests from many passengers who wished to
                              [make connections (50)
to other parts of the country. Yet, I must admit   (60)
to being aware that not all our patrons, particularly those   (70)
who are visiting the shopping precincts, find the new
                                   [terminus (80)
quite so convenient, and I hope to review the arrangements (90)
to see if any improvement can be made.
    Yours sincerely.   (100)

8 Dear Client,
    I would like to bring to your notice   (10)
our first-class insurance scheme which we are now able   (20)
to offer. This will protect you against sickness and accident (30)
and will also include full life cover.
    Under this scheme,   (40)
should you be unfortunate enough to become ill or the   (50)
victim of an accident, your monthly repayments will be
                                   [suspended, (60)
but will continue to be met by us.
    Because of   (70)
your past association with our company you can take
                                 [advantage (80)
of this scheme without undergoing a medical examination.
                                   [So, why (90)
not complete the enclosed approval form to enable your
                                [application (100)
to be treated with priority?
    Yours sincerely.   (107)

9 Doors which can be locked from the inside should have   (10)
bolts fitted at top and bottom in addition to a   (20)
secure lock. A spy hole or door chain gives a   (30)

view of any caller without the need for the door   *(40)*
to be opened more than a fraction. Never leave a   *(50)*
key in the lock or hidden under a mat when   *(60)*
going out.
    When the house is empty, do not risk   *(70)*
being burgled by leaving windows open, especially on the
                               [ground   *(80)*
floor or near drainpipes and extensions.
    Many people do not   *(90)*
realize that garden sheds and garages should also be locked   *(100)*
not only because of their contents, but also because they   *(110)*
often contain ladders and tools which the would-be burglar   *(120)*
might use to break in.   *(125)*

10 Dear Mr White,
    As one of our past customers, I   *(10)*
would like to thank you for the excellent way in   *(20)*
which your account has been conducted throughout the
                              [agreement. For   *(30)*
this reason I would now like to give you the   *(40)*
opportunity of applying for a further personal loan. This will   *(50)*
enable you to afford any particular item you have in   *(60)*
mind without a long delay.
    Any amount between five hundred   *(70)*
pounds and five thousand pounds will be sent to you   *(80)*
once your application has been accepted. Payments can be
                              [spread   *(90)*
over a term of five years if you so wish,   *(100)*
and I would draw your attention to the enclosed table   *(110)*
so that you can choose your repayments to fit in   *(120)*
with your budget.
    We look forward to hearing from you.   *(130)*
    Yours sincerely.   *(132)*

2 Distinguishing Outlines

Although the context of a passage will usually make the meaning of similarly written outlines clear, and vowels can be added for greater clarity, the following list has been compiled to help in distinguishing between words that might be confused in some circumstances. (See also Appendix 2 in *Teeline: Revised Edition*.)

There is no need to drill all these words, but where any appear in a passage being prepared for dictation, reference can be made to them.

adopt				adapt			
best	beset			beside		biased	
barrier				bearer			
case				cause			
censor				connoisseur			
daughter				debtor			
decision				discussion			
defence				defiance			
deter				detour			
economies				economize			
effect				affect			
emotion				emission			
exercise				exorcize			
farm				forum			
file				phial			

...⟋⟋⟍... garden	...⟋⟋⟍... guardian
...⟋⟍... impassioned	...⟋⟍... impatient
...⟍... inconstancy	...⟍... inconsistency
...⟍... ingenious	...⟍... ingenuous
...⟍... invasion	...⟍... innovation
...⟍... Mary	...⟍... Marie
...⟍... moral	...⟍... morale
...⟍... minister	...⟍... monster
...⟍... neatness	...⟍... neatens
...⟍... offhand	...⟍... offend
...⟍... overhead	...⟍... overheat
...⟍... peerless	...⟍... powerless
...⟍... people	...⟍... pupil
...⟍... poor	...⟍... pure
...⟍... poorest	...⟍... purest
...⟍... satin	...⟍... stone
...⟍... solitary	...⟍... sultry	...⟍... salutary
...⟍... sparse	...⟍... spurious
...⟍... stable	...⟍... suitable
...⟍... stood	...⟍... stayed
...⟍... studied	...⟍... stated

6

..... substance   ..... subsidence

..... support   ..... separate   ..... spirit

..... tact   ..... ticket

..... tour   ..... tower

..... *or* ..... unstable   ..... *or* ..... unsuitable

..... violation   ..... valuation

Groupings

Remember to distinguish between:

..... I would   ..... it would

..... you would   ..... we would

..... additional   ..... advisory   ..... advertising
    committee   committee   committee

..... before the   ..... by far the

..... expected markets   ..... export markets

..... rising unemployment   ..... rise in unemployment

..... take over   ..... take cover

Exercises

1 An additional committee was formed to help those in need   *(10)*
to take advantage of the facilities to which they were   *(20)*
entitled.   *(21)*

2 Mary was a poor singer but Marie's voice, though lacking   *(10)*
in power, was pure and sweet. They were both lovely   *(20)*
girls, but Mary was more lively than her elder sister.   *(30)*

7

3 Unable to show her defiance openly, she devised ingenious
[ways   (*10*)
of being disobedient. No one looking at her ingenuous
[expression (*20*)
would have guessed what a little monster she really was.   (*30*)

4 His offhand manner did not offend me as I realized   (*10*)
he was preoccupied with the problems of rising
[unemployment and (*20*)
with what would happen to the firm if their expected   (*30*)
markets failed to materialize.   (*34*)

5 After they had seen the film and studied various reports   (*10*)
on it, the committee agreed it would be unsuitable for   (*20*)
those who were emotionally unstable, so they decided to ban (*30*)
its showing in the city.   (*35*)

6 It is said that there is to be another discussion   (*10*)
about the effect on workers of spending long hours in   (*20*)
an overheated environment, but the fact is that no decisions (*30*)
ever seem to result from these discussions.   (*37*)

7 We now knew that the long spell of sultry weather   (*10*)
had affected the touring team and put paid to their   (*20*)
chances of becoming the champions. It was so hot that   (*30*)
any form of exercise quickly exhausted them.   (*37*)

8 To get from the farm to the Forum, it was   (*10*)
necessary for us to make a detour past the minister's   (*20*)
house. He was taking a stroll in the garden and   (*30*)
called out cheerfully to my guardian as we passed.   (*39*)

9 I imagine the rateable value of this property will have   (*10*)
to be lowered on account of the subsidence, but there   (*20*)
is no substance in the rumour that the council intend   (*30*)
to take over the house under a compulsory purchase order. (*40*)

10 I would be surprised if the home team beat the   (*10*)
visitors easily. Usually they have quite a struggle to draw (*20*)
but, of course, it would be a boost to their   (*30*)
morale if they did manage to win on this occasion.   (*40*)

11 The film censor has the reputation of being a connoisseur (*10*)
of good wine, but do not let this deter you (*20*)
from offering him a glass of your home-made variety (*30*)
before the evening is over. It is by far the (*40*)
best I have tasted for a long time. (*48*)

12 As the train drew into the station, I noticed a (*10*)
solitary girl wearing a satin blouse, which was not the (*20*)
most suitable attire for the time of the year. She (*30*)
stood beside the ticket barrier, eagerly watching the
[arriving passengers (*40*)
and I stayed to see for whom she was waiting. (*50*)

13 We must exercise our minds over the best way to (*10*)
exorcize the strange presence which is said to oppress people (*20*)
on their way to the tower. Two of our neighbours' (*30*)
daughters have reported hearing unusual noises overhead,
[but these could (*40*)
be due to an invasion of birds which commonly beset (*50*)
the neighbourhood during the nesting season. (*56*)

14 We would be very pleased if you would agree to (*10*)
take over the management of the canteen until we are (*20*)
able to make further arrangements. We understand that you
[wish (*30*)
to retire before the end of the year, but as (*40*)
long as you remain with the firm, you are by (*50*)
far the best person for the job. Could you let (*60*)
us know your decision within the next week if possible. (*70*)

3 The Contraction of Words: Part I

When a shorthand writer is capable of taking down notes at 80 words a minute or more, *and of reading them back with ease*, the attainment of a higher speed may be helped by contracting outlines. This should be done, however, with care, as haphazard abbreviating can cause difficulties and errors in transcription. A good rule to follow is: *If in doubt, write it out*, but it should be safe to adopt the following suggestions:

1 The omission of L in words ending in -LY

(Many examples of this appear in *Teeline: Revised Edition* – see the list of reduced outlines in Appendix 3.)

closely	continuously
correctly	firmly
historically	nicely
occasionally	personally
quickly	substantially
suddenly	unfortunately

Some exceptions

necessarily	(necessary)
momentarily	(momentary)
perfectly	(perfect)
strategically	(strategy)
conveniently	(convenient)
legitimately	(legitimate)

And in words using the -ABLE ending

...... ⌇ ...... capably   ...... ∿ ...... fashionably

...... ⌇ᴎ .... questionably   ...... ◌ᴎ ...... reasonably

2 The omission of N and L or NTL in words ending in -NTLY

...... ⌇ ..... consequently   ... ⌇ ..... *or* ..... ⌇ ...... consistently

.... ⌇ ...... *or* .... ⌇ .... constantly   .. ⌇ ...... inadvertently

..... ⌇ .... incidentally   ...... ⌇ .... independently
                              ⌇ (see also next section)

... ⌇ ...... instantly   ..... ⌇ .... *or* ...... ⌇ ... persistently

Some exceptions (words which are already contracted or special outlines)

... ⌇ .... deliberately   .... ⌇ ...... importantly

..... ⌇ .... recently   .... ⌇ ..... permanently

..... ⌇ ... prominently

Some writers may prefer to shorten words more than others. For instance,

   certainly may be written .... ⌇ ...... *or* .... ⌇ ....

   conspicuously may be written ..... ⌇ ...... *or* ... ⌇ ....

   democratically may be written ... ⌇ ..... *or* .. ⌇ ...

The test will be whether the word can be read back in context correctly.

3 The omission of N in words beginning with IND-

In Unit 25 of *Teeline: Revised Edition*, N is omitted in words beginning with INS- and INC-. This is an extension of that principle.

independent	indefatigable
indelible	indication
individual	indescribable
indispensable	indignation *or*
indolence	inducement
industrial	industrious
	(industries)

4 The omission of N in certain words before T

administer	alternate
alternately *or*	alternative
alternatively	delinquent
defendant	dependent/dependant
entertainment	inadvertent
inadvertently	inconsistent
inconsistently	

and in

arrange	arranged

12

....~~...... arrangement ....~~...... danger

....~~.... dangers ....~~.... dangerous

.... astronomer .... astronomy

.....~~... Manchester

5 In some word groupings the N can be omitted between OU or W and T or D

.....~~.... around the .....~~.... down the

.....~~.... between the .....~~... Lawn Tennis

Exercises

1 It is sometimes necessary to deal quickly and firmly with   (10)
  badly behaved individuals if one wishes to deter them from   (20)
  becoming delinquents.   (22)

2 Because the bridge was considered to be in a dangerous   (10)
  state, an alternative route to Manchester was arranged for all   (20)
  road traffic.   (22)

3 There is a precise difference between the words 'continually'
  [and   (10)
  'continuously'. If you do not know what it is, consult   (20)
  a dictionary.   (22)

4 An astronomer studies the stars and other heavenly bodies.
  [An   (10)
  astrologer tries to predict what influence they will have on   (20)
  human beings.   (22)

5 While the assistant's attention was momentarily distracted,
  [the shop-lifter   (10)
  quickly slipped one of the packets into her bag, not   (20)
  realizing that she was being closely watched by the store   (30)
  detective.   (31)

13

6 Generally he was a very careful driver, but when the (10)
car in front suddenly stopped, he realized he had been (20)
following it too closely and, unfortunately, he was unable to (30)
avoid bumping into it. (34)

7 Between the wars, the small, independent and democratically
[governed countries (10)
of Europe were continuously under threat of being overrun
[by (20)
the larger industrial nations who found it strategically
[advantageous to (30)
enlarge their geographical boundaries. (34)

8 The head typist found it necessary to complain constantly
[about (10)
the new girl's indolence. She told her that she would (20)
have to learn that certainly no one is indispensable and (30)
that if she did not apply herself she would have (40)
to leave. (42)

9 As I came down the road, I saw a large (10)
prominently displayed sign, nicely printed in indelible ink,
[pinned to (20)
the gates of the Lawn Tennis Club. Around this stood (30)
several individuals who appeared to be in a state of (40)
some indignation. (42)

10 Newspapers occasionally run competitions as an inducement
[for people to (10)
buy them. Cars, luxury cruises or cash alternatives are
[offered (20)
and some readers are firmly convinced that they will win (30)
one of these prizes. Others simply see the games as (40)
a form of entertainment. (44)

11 Many members of the public derive much enjoyment from
[watching (10)
tennis. Some individuals win by playing the ball
[strategically. Others (20)
are good sometimes but play inconsistently and a few
[inadvertently (30)

or deliberately provide entertainment. Most people deplore
[the fact that (40)
occasionally there are displays of temper and bad
[sportsmanship, but (50)
the inducement of large cash prizes for the winners may (60)
have something to do with the deterioration in behaviour. (69)

12 Many householders today are firmly committed to following
[the latest (10)
fashion trend for fitted units and furniture, and to disposing (20)
of their free-standing individual pieces. Initially, basic units
[can (30)
be quickly fitted into convenient recesses at very low cost, (40)
leading on to far more sophisticated and perfectly styled
[arrangements (50)
in all shapes and sizes as money becomes available. Bank (60)
loans are generally obtainable to assist in such improvement
[projects. (70)

4 The Contraction of Words: Part II

1 The joining of -TION following T, TR, D and DR

In order to eliminate a hand movement, the disjoined N for -TION may be joined to a preceding T, D, TR or DR.

_...._ concentration instead of _...._

_...._ condition instead of _...._

_...._ consideration instead of _...._

_...._ hesitation instead of _...._

Practise the following:

_...._ administration

_...._ arbitration

_...._ confederation

_...._ *or* _...._ confrontation
(The N is also omitted)

_...._ demonstration

_...._ expedition

_...._ extradition

_...._ *or* _...._ infiltration

_...._ malnutrition

_...._ moderation

_...._ nutritional

_...._ penetration

_...._ reputation

_...._ restoration

_...._ saturation

_...._ situation

_...._ unconstitutional

Outlines where the -TION is not joined

_...._ deterioration

_...._ misrepresentation

...... assassination

Distinguishing outlines

...... contrition   ...... contortion

Words ending in -MENTATION have the -TION joined to the disjoined MENT

...... documentation   ...... fomentation

...... fragmentation   ...... implementation

...... lamentation   ...... ornamentation

...... regimentation

2 The contraction of long words

These may be shortened by:

(a) Leaving out the middle of the word

...... circumstantial   ...... embankment

...... generalization   ...... henceforth

...... imperturbable   ...... impracticable

...... investigation   ...... organization

...... pandemonium   ...... perforation

...... preliminary   ...... unquestionably

...... victimization

(b) Leaving off the end of the word

...... advantage   ...... deliberate

...... improbable   ...... insubordination

17

..... ⌢ᴍ .... quantity   ..... ⌁ᴛ̅⌒ᴏ̅ ..... re-establish

.... tomorrow   .... ⌣ᴜ .... yesterday

Special outline

... ⌁ᴠᴧ ..... disadvantage (The D is also omitted)

Exercises

1 Every form of government has its advantages and
                                  [disadvantages, but *(10)*
  even in a democratically run society, there is bound to *(20)*
  be some regimentation. *(23)*

2 My concentration was only momentarily diverted from the
                                        [screen but *(10)*
  it was long enough to cause me to miss what *(20)*
  I had been waiting to see. *(26)*

3 Preliminary investigation has revealed some inconsistency
                          [in the defendants' stories *(10)*
  and the reputation of the firm is unquestionably at stake *(20)*
  until the matter is cleared up. *(26)*

4 An investigation into the demonstration on the
                         [Embankment last Saturday *(10)*
  revealed that some individuals had deliberately
                         [attempted to create pandemonium. *(20)*
  Naturally, they complained of victimization when brought
                         [to court. *(29)*

5 Allegations of the misrepresentation of the facts by the
                         [Press *(10)*
  has brought a serious deterioration in the situation. It is *(20)*
  difficult to establish the truth, but there is talk of *(30)*
  the case going to arbitration. *(35)*

6 Demonstrations are held regularly by many organizations
                         [against regimentation or *(10)*

victimization in some form or another. Unquestionably

[they have a *(20)*
right to make their protest, so long as pandemonium does *(30)*
not ensue and law and order are maintained. *(38)*

7 The application of hot fomentations to swellings used to be *(10)*
a common method of relieving the pain, but today we *(20)*
know that the main cause of the trouble may lie *(30)*
in the general condition of the patients, who may be *(40)*
suffering from a nutritional deficiency. *(45)*

8 For various reasons, many people in underdeveloped

[countries suffer from *(10)*
malnutrition. Sometimes it is because of indescribable

[poverty, and sometimes *(20)*
because of bad organization. Aid sent often does not reach *(30)*
those in need because of inefficient administration. This

[must be *(40)*
a cause of lamentation to the sufferers. *(47)*

9 The Confederation of British Industries, more commonly

[referred to as *(10)*
the C.B.I., is one of the bodies which *(20)*
regularly offers advice to the government. The

[implementation of its *(30)*
suggestions does not necessarily follow, since it does not

[possess *(40)*
any powers of confrontation which organizations of

[employees enjoy. *(49)*

10 The recreation committee has made a preliminary

[investigation into the *(10)*
possibility of re-establishing the Athletics Club. Many

[members of *(20)*
the public have deliberately formed a pressure group to

[bring *(30)*
about the club's restoration, in the hope that henceforth the *(40)*
young people will be able to take advantage of the *(50)*
facilities it will offer. *(54)*

5 Prefixes and Suffixes

In addition to the Word Beginnings and Endings already listed in *Teeline: Revised Edition*, the use of the following may assist in reducing the length of outlines.

Prefixes

1 ANTA-/ANTE-/ANTI-

Write a disjoined AN in the T position ....

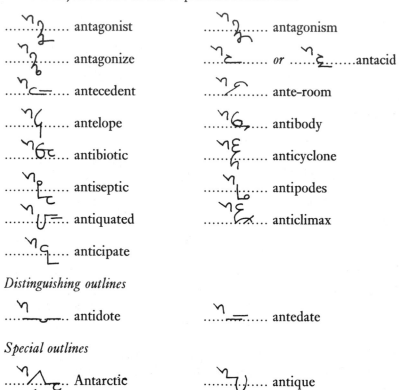

.... antagonist

.... antagonism

.... antagonize

.... *or* .... antacid

.... antecedent

.... ante-room

.... antelope

.... antibody

.... antibiotic

.... anticyclone

.... antiseptic

.... antipodes

.... antiquated

.... anticlimax

.... anticipate

Distinguishing outlines

.... antidote

.... antedate

Special outlines

.... Antarctic

.... antique

2 ULTRA-

Write a disjoined full U on the line ...U.........

.... ultra-modern

.... ultramarine

20

...ᴜᴄ̲... ultra-violet   ...ᴜ2... ultrasonic

...ᴜᴧ... ultra-fashionable   ...ᴜᴄᴧ... ultramicroscope

3 HYPER-

Write a disjoined HPR ....|ᴠ........

...|ᴄᴠ... hyperactive   ....|ᴠᴄ.... hyperbole

...|ᴧ...... hypertension   ...|ᴄᴄ... *or* ...|ᴄ...... hypercritical

...|ᴅᴠ. hypersensitive

Special outline

....|ᴧ.... hypermarket

4 HYPO-

Write a disjoined HYP ...ʮ.........

...ʮ——ᴄ hypodermic   ..ʮᴄᴄ... hypochondriac

..ʮᴅ...... hypothesis   ..ʮᴧ...... hypotenuse

....ʮᴄ...... hypocrite   ..ʮᴧ.. hypothermia

Exercises

1 An ultramicroscope is an instrument under which objects
                         [too small   (*10*)
   to be seen with an ordinary microscope can be studied.   (*20*)

2 It is a sad reflection on our present–day society   (*10*)
   that each year many old people die of hypothermia because   (*20*)
   they cannot afford to keep warm.   (*26*)

3 It is important to distinguish between 'hypercritical' and
                    ['hypocritical'. A   (*10*)
   hypercritical person constantly finds fault, but is not
                    [necessarily guilty   (*20*)

21

of hypocrisy, and hypocrites may be very tolerant towards

                          [others. *(30)*

4 In accordance with the ultra-modern fashion of the day,   *(10)*
  one wall of the room was painted ultramarine, in contrast   *(20)*
  to the other three, and this colour was echoed in   *(30)*
  several of the cushions scattered about.   *(36)*

5 Many of the more valuable antiques in the exhibition were   *(10)*
  displayed in an ante-room where tight security could more   *(20)*
  easily be maintained. It was an interesting thought that these   *(30)*
  antiquated items had once again become ultra-fashionable.   *(38)*

6 Many mothers today complain that their children are

                    [hyperactive. One *(10)*
  hypothesis for this phenomenon is that many of today's

                        [processed *(20)*
  foods contain chemicals which act like a drug on young   *(30)*
  people and stimulate them to over-activity.   *(37)*

7 The Australian weather forecaster announced that because an

                    [anticyclone near *(10)*
  the Antarctic was moving in the direction of New Zealand,   *(20)*
  a change in the weather for the State of Victoria   *(30)*
  could be anticipated in the next few days.   *(38)*

8 There was much antagonism from the medical profession

                    [towards the *(10)*
  use of antiseptics when this discovery was first made. Today   *(20)*
  there is some evidence to suggest that doctors accept new   *(30)*
  discoveries far too readily and they have been criticized

                           [for *(40)*
  making too much use of antibiotics in treating their patients.   *(50)*

Suffixes

1 -AVITY/-EVITY

Write a disjoined V in the T position .... ⌄

.... grave but .... gravity

.... cave but .... cavity

.... deprave but .... depravity

.... levity   .... brevity   .... longevity

2 -PATH

Write a disjoined P ....

.... osteopath   .... naturopath

.... psychopath

-PATHY

Write a disjoined PY ....

.... antipathy   .... sympathy

.... empathy   .... homoeopathy

.... telepathy

-PATHIC

Write a disjoined PIC ....

.... telepathic   .... psychopathic

-PATHICALLY

Write a disjoined PICY ....

.... homoeopathically

Special outlines

.... apathy   .... apathetic

.... pathetic   .... pathetically

.... sympathetic   .... sympathetically

.... unsympathetic   .... unsympathetically

Exercises

1 This is a situation of the utmost gravity and I   *(10)*
  am surprised to find it being treated with such levity.   *(20)*

2 One would expect telepathic people to be blessed with a   *(10)*
  sensitivity and empathy which make them receptive to other
                                                        [people's   *(20)*
  thoughts and feelings.   *(23)*

3 Homoeopathy is becoming very popular. This is the
                                        [treatment of   *(10)*
  illness by administering minute doses of medicines which,
                                            [if taken   *(20)*
  in larger quantities, would be dangerous. It is reported that   *(30)*
  the Queen has a homoeopathic doctor among her physicians.   *(39)*

4 Giving evidence, the psychiatrist stated that the accused
                                      [frequently reacted   *(10)*
  violently to anyone who antagonized him, but he could not   *(20)*
  say at this stage whether the accused had psychopathic
                                          [tendencies   *(30)*
  or whether he was suffering from bouts of hypertension
                                            [which   *(40)*
  affected his behaviour.   *(43)*

5 The young are often accused of being apathetic and it   *(10)*
  is true that some of them admit to being bored,   *(20)*
  but it is also true that a great many show   *(30)*
  much sympathetic concern for those less fortunate than
                                          [themselves and   *(40)*
  do valuable work in raising money for charity.   *(48)*

6 An osteopath treats bone and muscle defects by manipulation
                                          [rather   *(10)*
  than by surgery and a naturopath treats illness by using   *(20)*
  natural remedies rather than drugs. One could go to either   *(30)*
  or both for a condition like arthritis but, unfortunately, in   *(40)*
  this country, such services are not yet part of the   *(50)*

National Health Service, so they tend to be expensive. Most   *(60)*
people, therefore, carry on in the traditional way and

                        [continue   *(70)*

to consult a doctor when they are ill.   *(78)*

6 Words ending in -NGE

Just as a disjoined vowel indicator represents the word endings -ANG, -ING, -ONG and -UNG, so a disjoined G may be used to represent the word endings -ANGE, -INGE, -ONGE and -UNGE, instead of writing N and G as previously.

-ANGE	......⌐ŋ......	instead of ....⌐ŋ......	for change
-INGE	....ɓ.ŋ.....	instead of ....ɓ........	for binge
-ONGE	.....P.ŋ......	instead of ......P........	for sponge
-UNGE	.....Ϥŋ.....	instead of ....Ϥŋ........	for lunge

Practise the following:

-ANGE   ....ŋ... strange   ....ɔ⫽.. stranger

..........⌢.ŋ... mange   ......⌢.ŋ... mangy

......⌢ŋ⫽. manger   ....ŋ... derange

....ℓ.ŋ..... flange   ..ɓŋ....... blancmange

Special outlines

...—ŋ⫽.... danger   ...—ŋℓ.... dangers

...—ŋᴌℓ.. dangerous (see page 13)

-INGE   ....ɭŋ..... hinge   ....↗ŋ..... fringe

......ɑŋ..... singe   ....ᴄℓŋ... cringe

..........ŋ.. twinge   ....↗ŋŋ..... impinge

.......—ŋ... dingy

-ONGE/-OUNGE ......Ϥᴗŋ.. lounge   ...Ϥᴗŋ⫽.. lounger

..... scrounge

-UNGE ..... plunge ..... dungeon

-ENGE ..... Stonehenge ..... Penge

Exercises

1 Real sponges are living things which must be harvested
[from *(10)*
the sea, so they are more expensive than manufactured
[sponges. *(20)*

2 Descending into the dungeon, the soldiers found the
[prisoner cringing *(10)*
in a corner in an apparently deranged state of mind. *(20)*

3 Stonehenge is a circle of stones in the southern part *(10)*
of Britain where it is believed that strange religious rites *(20)*
were once practised. *(23)*

4 The sight of the mangy dog, crouching by the manger *(10)*
threw everyone momentarily into a panic, but it soon ran *(20)*
off and plunged into the nearby river. *(27)*

5 The hinge was broken and made the strangest of banging *(10)*
noises whenever the office door was opened, thus causing
[everyone *(20)*
sitting inside to cringe at the sound. *(27)*

6 The representative did not wish to impinge on the manager's *(10)*
free time, so suggested a visit might be arranged to *(20)*
coincide with part of the lunch break. *(27)*

7 As the lounge was rather dingy, it was decided to *(10)*
give the woodwork a new coat of paint and to *(20)*
change the curtains for some with a brighter coloured design. *(30)*

8 One of the fringe benefits of a secluded garden is *(10)*
the privacy it gives on hot sunny days when one *(20)*
can laze in a deck chair or sun lounger without *(30)*
being overlooked. *(32)*

7 The Contraction of Word Groupings

1 The omission of words

(a) The omission of the word A

.... in (a) way .... as (a) rule

.... in (a) minute .... in (a) word

.... for (a) long time .... as (a) result

(b) The omission of the word AND

.... this (and) that .... here (and) there

.... up (and) down .... trade (and) industry

.... rank (and) file .... more (and) more

Special groupings

.... on and off .... men and women

.... ladies and gentlemen

(c) The omission of OF and OF THE

.... out (of the) question .... in support (of)

.... state (of) things .... sign (of the) times

.... present state (of) .... rate (of) interest

.... Secretary (of) State .... Secretary (of) State (for) Education

.... at the end (of the) day .... cause (of the) accident

(d) The omission of the word TO

.... according (to) the .... ought (to) have

.... seems (to) have .... enabled (to)
       been

.... in addition (to) .... times (to) come

(e) The omission of THE or TO THE

.... on (the) subject (of) .... came (to the) conclusion

.... in (the) first place .... in (the) second place

.... in (the) hands of .... owing (to the) fact that

Exercises

1 Although there have been several investigations into the

                                                     [advantages and *(10)*
    disadvantages of the comprehensive school, at the end of the *(20)*
    day, the matter is in the hands of the Secretary *(30)*
    of State for Education. *(34)*

2 It is a sign of the times that for a *(10)*
    long time the figures released by the Departments of Trade *(20)*
    and Industry have shown a steady rise in the number *(30)*
    of firms being forced to make staff redundant or to *(40)*
    close down. *(42)*

3 While we are on the subject of organization, I have *(10)*
    been meaning to ask you for a long time if *(20)*
    you can estimate how many extra men and women we *(30)*
    shall need to staff the new administrative block when it *(40)*
    is ready. *(42)*

4 Unquestionably, there is a great deal of circumstantial

                                                       [evidence in *(10)*
    support of your theory but, in the first place, we *(20)*
    have not yet established where our suspect was yesterday
                                                          [and *(30)*

in the second place, whether he was in a condition (40)
to commit such a crime. (45)

5 As a rule, we often put a task off till (10)
tomorrow when we could do it today. We very often (20)
promise to see to matters 'in a minute' but, unfortunately, (30)
that minute never seems to arrive and when tomorrow
[comes (40)
some individuals are still catching up with yesterday's work. (49)

2 Special groupings

The following words may be contracted in groupings only:

(a) CITY – This may be shown as **CY in the T position**: ....

.... City of Birmingham   .... Nottingham City

.... City of London   .... City and Guilds

.... The City

(b) INDUSTRY – This may be contracted **by omitting the**

IN: ....

.... building industry   .... fishing industry

.... British industry   .... mining industry

(c) COMMITTEE – This may be contracted to ITE ....

.... strike committee   .... management
committee

.... finance committee   .... general purposes
committee

(d) ROYAL – This may be contracted to ROY ....

.... Royal Commission   .... Royal Family

30

.... Royal Yacht   .... Royal Borough

.... Royal Train   .... Royal Tour

(e) ASSOCIATION – This may be contracted to ASN ....

.... Teeline Association   .... Family Planning Association

.... Association of Small Shopkeepers   .... Association of Fair Trading

.... Memorandum of Association   .... Articles of Association

Exercises

1 The fishing industry has been badly hit by the implementation (10)
of laws which limit the areas where fishing is allowed (20)
and the weight of the catches. (26)

2 According to the strike committee, workers in British
[industry were (10)
not getting a fair deal compared to their counterparts in (20)
Europe, but the management committee disagreed with
[this statement. (29)

3 The City of Nottingham is well-known in many parts (10)
of the world because of its association with Robin Hood, (20)
a legendary figure who was said to have lived in (30)
Sherwood Forest, which once surrounded the city. (37)

4 'The City' is a term commonly used to cover the (10)
banks and other financial institutions, such as the Stock
[Exchange, (20)
in the City of London. Such expressions as 'The City (30)
reacted favourably to the news' may often be heard on (40)
radio broadcasts. (42)

5 There is always much interest among the general public, both (10)
at home and abroad, in the activities of the Royal (20)

Family and when a Royal Tour is in progress, the   (30)
popular newspapers are full of reports and pictures, which
                                                [make (40)
a pleasant change from the usual depressing news items.   (49)

3 OR or R in groupings

(a) Sometimes an R stroke can be substituted for the word OR

.... some time or other   .... men or women

.... this or that   .... somehow or other

(b) Sometimes the word OR is omitted altogether

.... one (or) two   .... three (or) four

.... more (or) less   .... whether (or) not

(c) If OR or R follows T, it can be shown by writing a TR stroke

.... right or wrong   .... first-rate

.... shorthand writer   .... shorthand writing

(The word HAND is also omitted in the last two groupings.)

4 The omission of T

where it is only lightly sounded

.... almost impossible   .... most important

.... past year

(Notice how the P slopes in the A direction in the last grouping
above.)

5 The use of one consonant to do the work of two

.... better *r*esults   .... hard*l*y *l*ikely

..... some *measure*   ..... this *statement*

..... pe*c*uliar *c*ircumstances   ..... pe*c*uliar *c*ircumstances of the case

..... use*d* *t*o be   ..... some *m*oney

..... par*t*-*t*ime   ..... ta*k*e *k*indly

6 The contraction of ENQUIRY/INQUIRY by the omission of R

..... your enquiry   ..... letter of enquiry

..... full inquiry   ..... several inquiries

..... preliminary enquiry   ..... line of inquiry

Exercises

1 A preliminary inquiry revealed one or two peculiar
     [circumstances, so   (*10*)
the Secretary of State ordered a full inquiry into the   (*20*)
matter.   (*21*)

2 During the past three or four years there has been   (*10*)
a great change in attitudes to sex equality and now   (*20*)
most jobs are open to both men and women.   (*29*)

3 If you wish to become a first-rate shorthand writer,   (*10*)
it is most important that you spend some time in   (*20*)
study each day during the learning period, whether or not   (*30*)
you feel like working.   (*34*)

4 We have had several enquiries during the past year from   (*10*)
both men and women wishing to join the firm as   (*20*)
directors. The last letter of enquiry came from a well-   (*30*)
known leader of industry. We are hardly likely to receive   (*40*)
a more suitable application than this.   (*46*)

7 Some groupings using WORDS

.... in other words   .... in their words

.... in his words   .... in his own words

.... (a) few words   .... common words

.... in the words (of)   .... the exact words

.... in your own words   .... words a minute

         (............... w.a.m.)

8 The contraction of REQUIRE/REQUIRED/ REQUIREMENT by the omission of R

.... your requirements   .... will you require

.... what is required   .... urgently required

9 The contraction of BEGINNING to GN

.... from the beginning   .... in the beginning

.... at the beginning   .... from beginning to end

.... beginning (to) see   .... beginning (to) think

.... beginning (to) rain

10 THAN and ON groupings

THAN may be reduced **by omitting the T**

.... nearer than   .... rather than

.... further than   .... farther than

.... later than   .... higher than

34

..... greater than ..... sooner than

ON may be reduced to N only

..... later on ..... carry on

..... take on

Distinguishing outlines

..... farther on ..... further on

Special groupings

..... more than ..... bigger than

..... smaller than ..... put on

..... press on

Exercises

1 We have appealed against the Corporation Tax assessment.
 [It is *(10)*
much higher than it should be and there are one *(20)*
or two expenses from the past year which should have *(30)*
been taken into account. *(34)*

2 We are hardly likely to achieve better results if we *(10)*
do not take some measures to eliminate the factors which *(20)*
contributed to our lack of success during the past year. *(30)*
Somehow or other, we must try to persuade the finance *(40)*
committee to allocate more money to this new project. *(49)*

3 I am beginning to think that we should take on *(10)*
a few more part-time workers, or it will be *(20)*
almost impossible to fulfil these orders. Will you have a *(30)*
few words with the Managing Director about the matter and *(40)*
let me know later on today what he says? *(49)*

4 The rate of interest paid by the banks is sometimes   (*10*)
  a little lower than that paid by the building societies   (*20*)
  and sometimes a little higher, but investors are hardly likely   (*30*)
  to leave their money where it is earning them one   (*40*)
  or two per cent per annum less, and will move   (*50*)
  their money to where they can obtain the best rates.   (*60*)

5 Dear Sir,
  We were pleased to receive your enquiry of   (*10*)
  yesterday's date, as we were beginning to think that you   (*20*)
  had decided not to place an order with us. If   (*30*)
  you can let us know as soon as possible exactly   (*40*)
  what your requirements are, we will do our best to   (*50*)
  get the goods to you before the end of the   (*60*)
  month.
    Yours faithfully.   (*63*)

8 Negatives

1 Words beginning with IN-

.... inaction

.... incompetent

.... inhuman

.... or .... inflexible

.... incomplete

.... inaccessible

.... incapable

.... inaccurate

.... inadmissible

.... incautious

.... inapplicable

Exercises

1 The reason for all the inaction at the works was *(10)*
because the operatives were incapable of working in such a *(20)*
hot environment. *(22)*

2 Obviously, the members of staff concerned are incompetent
[because this *(10)*
is the third time this month that the figures have *(20)*
been incomplete. *(22)*

3 The evidence was inadmissible and the judge would have
[been *(10)*
thought most inhuman and inflexible if he had allowed it *(20)*
to be considered. *(23)*

4 Because the excavations are, as yet, incomplete, and safety
[measures *(10)*
are inadequate, it would be incautious to attempt any further *(20)*
work on the site. *(24)*

5 We spent a considerable time searching for the papers which *(10)*
were almost inaccessible at the bottom of the pile, and *(20)*
when they did eventually come to light, the information, far *(30)*
from being helpful, was quite inapplicable. *(36)*

37

2 Words beginning with IM-

...... impossible

...... impassable

...... immaterial

...... impatience

...... improbable

...... impure

...... impatient

...... impracticable

...... immobile

... *or* ... immovable

Exercises

1 It is highly improbable that the water is impure as   (*10*)
  checks for pollution are made daily.   (*16*)

2 It is immaterial that these laboratory tests were inconclusive,
                                                              [but (*10*)
  we await the other results with impatience.   (*17*)

3 There is no point in being impatient. However long the   (*10*)
  delay, it is impracticable to bypass the normal channels.   (*19*)

4 Without the use of his car, the representative was immobile   (*10*)
  but the magistrate remained immovable on the question of
                                                    [restoring (*20*)
  his licence.   (*22*)

5 The heavy seas made driving impossible on the coast road   (*10*)
  and it was expected that the road would remain impassable   (*20*)
  until daylight.   (*22*)

3 Words beginning with DIS-

...disconnected

...... displeased

...... discontinue

...... discontinued

...... discomfort

...... discontent

.... dishonest   .... discredit

.... disqualified   .... disbelief

.... disorderly

Exercises

1 The telephone will be disconnected immediately as the new
                                        [householder *(10)*
   has said he wishes to discontinue the rental.   *(18)*

2 The headmaster was displeased when he saw how much
                                        [discredit   *(10)*
   would be brought upon the school by the adverse report *(20)*
   in the local press.   *(24)*

3 During the hot weather, the dog appeared to be in   *(10)*
   a state of discomfort and expressed his discontent by snapping *(20)*
   at everyone who approached.   *(24)*

4 I looked at the monthly statement with horror and disbelief. *(10)*
   Surely no one on the staff could be so dishonest   *(20)*
   as to falsify the totals.   *(25)*

5 In addition to imposing a heavy fine for being drunk   *(10)*
   and disorderly, it was not surprising that the court also *(20)*
   disqualified the young man from driving for two years.   *(29)*

4 Words beginning with UN-

.... unhappiness   .... uncommon

.... unattainable   (........... untenable)

.... unkind   .... unapproachable

.... unwind   .... uncomfortable

.... unused   .... unsafe

39

.... unfortunately   .... unprecedented

.... unavailable   .... unable (to)

.... unavoidable   (....... inevitable)

Special outlines

.... unkind   .... unnecessary

Exercises

1 Is unhappiness simply a state of mind? Probably so, because   (*10*)
  happiness is sure to elude us when we strive for   (*20*)
  the unattainable.   (*22*)

2 In certain parts of the country, it is not uncommon   (*10*)
  to see a white blackbird. The lack of colour is   (*20*)
  caused by some mutation which means that the bird is   (*30*)
  unable to manufacture the necessary colouring pigment.   (*37*)

3 Until I became used to the ways of my neighbour   (*10*)
  I thought him unkind and unapproachable, but I know now   (*20*)
  that he is a very reserved individual who is always   (*30*)
  uncomfortable and unable to unwind in the presence of   (*40*)
                                                  [strangers.

5 Words beginning with IRRE-

.... irresistible   .... irreparable

.... irretrievably   .... irrecoverable

.... irregular   .... irresolute

.... irrational   .... irredeemable

.... irresponsible   .... irrelevant

Exercises

1 To even consider having a discussion without a quorum was   *(10)*
highly irregular, but if the members had not been so   *(20)*
irresolute, some headway could have been made.   *(27)*

2 I knew the Chairman was behaving in an irrational way,   *(10)*
but if he had given his casting vote, at least   *(20)*
the situation would not have been irredeemable.   *(27)*

3 I thought the tennis balls were irretrievably lost in the   *(10)*
hedge, but to my joy they were not irrecoverable as   *(20)*
we found them in an easily accessible spot.   *(28)*

4 On a hot summer day the attraction of water is   *(10)*
irresistible to small children, but irreparable damage to
[their confidence   *(20)*
may be caused if they inadvertently fall in, so careful   *(30)*
supervision is essential.   *(33)*

5 It may seem an irresponsible idea to sail single-handed   *(10)*
across the ocean, but this is irrelevant compared to the   *(20)*
sense of achievement experienced by the individual
[concerned, on reaching   *(30)*
the other shore.   *(33)*

9 Words Containing Joinings With S and Z

...... *access* ...... *assassin* ...... *assess*

...... *assist* ...... *assistance* ...... *assistant*

...... *basis* ...... *cease* ...... *census*

...... *disaster* ...... *disease* ...... *emphasis*

...... *excess* ...... *insist* ...... *possess*

...... *recess* ...... *recesses* ...... *resist*

...... *sausage* ...... *or* ...... *scissors*

...... *season* ...... *sister* ...... *or* ...... *size*

...... *or* ...... *society* ...... *success*

...... *suspect* ...... *sustain* ...... *system*

Exercises

1 Prevention is better than cure so, in the first place,   *(10)*
  emphasis should be on building up resistance against disease. *(19)*

2 The basis of success is said to be hard work   *(10)*
  but I suspect that luck and opportunity assist in sustaining *(20)*
  it. *(21)*

3 The shop assistant had been popular with the staff and   *(10)*
  they had a presentation to wish her every success in *(20)*
  her new career. *(23)*

4 It is claimed that wool carpets have more resistance to   *(10)*
  dirt and dust than synthetic fibres and are thus *(20)*
  easier to keep clean successfully. *(25)*

42

5 The assassins took advantage of the chaos caused by the   *(10)*
  rail disaster to seize the young kidnap victim who was   *(20)*
  in no position to resist.   *(25)*

6 The office staff quickly seized on the idea of disposing   *(10)*
  of the excess files which had ceased to be in   *(20)*
  regular use. The method of disposal used, of course, was   *(30)*
  shredding.   *(31)*

7 With the aid of a small pair of scissors, I   *(10)*
  managed to turn the key in the lock and free   *(20)*
  my sister who had been unable to resist the temptation   *(30)*
  of hiding in the cupboard recess.   *(36)*

8 The management wished to emphasize that, despite the
                     [apparent sales   *(10)*
  success and the size of the order book, it had   *(20)*
  been decided to cease production at the Subsidiary
                     [Company and   *(30)*
  to transfer the excess machinery and manpower to the main   *(40)*
  factory.   *(41)*

9 E.E.C. regulations mean that the traditional British sausage   *(10)*
  as we know it, may soon disappear. Food experts insist   *(20)*
  that the size and meat content should both be subject   *(30)*
  to legislation to bring the sausage into line with its   *(40)*
  continental counterpart.   *(42)*

10 Census returns have been compiled in Britain since
                     [eighteen-hundred-   *(10)*
  and-one and form the basis of much statistical information.   *(20)*
  They are accessible to the public after one hundred years   *(30)*
  and from them we are able to assess what society   *(40)*
  and the social system were like in the last century.   *(50)*
  The returns do not tell us how susceptible all classes   *(60)*
  of society were to disease or how little physical resistance   *(70)*
  they had, but much information can be sought out from   *(80)*
  contemporary accounts written by people who survived such
                     [epidemics and   *(90)*
  other disasters.   *(92)*

10 Acronyms and Abbreviations

Because Teeline is streamlined longhand, it is possible to make use of any longhand abbreviations which would normally be used in writing. We live in an age of abbreviations, many of which are understood even though the words for which they stand have been forgotten.

Sets of initials may, of course, have different meanings depending upon the context in which they are used. P.S. at the end of a letter is readily translated as 'postscript' but to a police officer it may suggest 'Police Sergeant' while to others it could mean 'Press Secretary', 'Private Secretary' or 'Privy Seal'. (See Unit 32, *Teeline: Revised Edition*.)

The word LIMITED may be written in full in Teeline ...⌐‿‿....

or reduced to its longhand abbreviation Ltd ....⌐⸗.... .

Similarly, the word COMPANY may be written in full ....⌐ᒇ.......

or as Co. ..⌐ᵥ......... .

Writing speed may be increased if a list of the commonly used words or groupings required in a particular job is compiled and a dictionary of longhand abbreviations studied to discover short ways of representing them. Provided these can be written quickly and read back accurately, it may be a safer method of abbreviating than over-contracting the standard Teeline outline.

List of acronyms and abbreviations used in the following exercises

......𝒷...... FIFO (first in, first out)

....ᴜ.ε.ʌ... UCCA (Universities' Central Council on Admissions)

.........ᒐ... ILEA (Inner London Education Authority)

....ᑧᵛ...... N.U.T. (National Union of Teachers)

......ᒿ𝒷...... NATFHE (National Association of Teachers in Further and Higher Education)

...⟨shorthand⟩... ACAS (Advisory, Conciliation and Arbitration Services)

...⟨shorthand⟩... radar (radio detection and ranging)   ...⟨shorthand⟩... Giro

...⟨shorthand⟩... FORTRAN ...⟨shorthand⟩... ALGOL ...⟨shorthand⟩... BASIC

...⟨shorthand⟩... ADA   ...⟨shorthand⟩... PASCAL

...⟨shorthand⟩... D.I.Y. (do it yourself)   ...⟨shorthand⟩... COBOL

...⟨shorthand⟩... C.C.P. (credit card purchase)

...⟨shorthand⟩... S.A.Y.E. (save as you earn)

The following short list of abbreviations do not appear in the exercises but may be useful for reference and to form the basis of individual lists:

...⟨shorthand⟩... al fresco   ...⟨shorthand⟩... *et al.*

...⟨shorthand⟩... bona fide   ...⟨shorthand⟩... e.g.

...⟨shorthand⟩... *et seq.*   ...⟨shorthand⟩... Ibid.

...⟨shorthand⟩... pro forma   ...⟨shorthand⟩... i.e.

...⟨shorthand⟩... q.v.   ...⟨shorthand⟩... quid pro quo

...⟨shorthand⟩... per capita   ...⟨shorthand⟩... *sic*

...⟨shorthand⟩... *sine die*   ...⟨shorthand⟩... viz

...⟨shorthand⟩... viva voca

Exercises

1 During times of industrial disputes, much is heard of the   *(10)*
  Conciliatory Service ACAS being called upon to intervene.   *(18)*

2 In any form of stocktaking the principle of FIFO is   *(10)*
  observed as it ensures that the oldest stock is always   *(20)*
  used up first.   *(23)*

3 Schools in such inter-city areas as ILEA have quite   *(10)*
a reputation for roughness and toughness but despite this a   *(20)*
high proportion of their students are still law-abiding.   *(29)*

4 The University Central Council on Admissions is known
[as UCCA.   *(10)*
As soon as the qualifying exam results are known, students   *(20)*
are offered places through UCCA, which acts as a central   *(30)*
clearing-house.   *(32)*

5 The N.U.T. is the largest teaching union in   *(10)*
Britain. Other teaching unions such as NATFHE are
[affiliated to   *(20)*
it because their executives feel that members' interests are
[better   *(30)*
served by so doing.   *(34)*

6 COBOL, FORTRAN, ALGOL and BASIC are computer
[languages which are   *(10)*
in common use. Several new computer languages, such as
[ADA   *(20)*
and PASCAL have now been devised which will help to   *(30)*
meet any future developments in the computing field.   *(38)*

7 Radar is derived from the phrase 'radio detection and
[ranging'   *(10)*
to denote the process of detecting distant objects by means   *(20)*
of radio wave echoes. Although initially a wartime device,
[the   *(30)*
uses of radar in peacetime are as numerous and important   *(40)*
as in war.   *(43)*

8 One job within easy reach of the D.I.Y.   *(10)*
enthusiast is that of building a garden pool. Once the   *(20)*
pool has been sunk, it is a comparatively simple matter   *(30)*
to activate the water by fitting a pump, so that   *(40)*
fish can be introduced. When all the work is completed,   *(50)*
the sight of fish swimming is an excellent way of   *(60)*
relaxing while deciding what the next D.I.Y. job   *(70)*
will be.   *(72)*

9 It is now possible for National Girobank customers to make (*10*)
payment into an overseas Giro account. Any sum can be (*20*)
transferred in the currency of the country concerned and
[there (*30*)
is no fee for international transfer credits. Giro transfers are (*40*)
an easy and cheap way of making payments abroad. The (*50*)
service is available free of charge and can be identified (*60*)
by the words Giro, Post Giro or C.C.P. (*70*)
before a Giro account number in newspaper and magazine
[advertisements. (*80*)

10 A good method of regular saving is to agree to (*10*)
have a specific sum deducted from your earnings. It is (*20*)
well named as S.A.Y.E. or Save As (*30*)
You Earn, because the amount to be saved is taken (*40*)
out of your wage or salary by your employer once (*50*)
you enter into a National Savings Contract. The
[government guarantees (*60*)
to protect your money from inflation for a period of (*70*)
five years from the commencement of the contract and
[offers (*80*)
even better returns if you then leave the money for (*90*)
a further two years after the payments have ceased. S. (*100*)
A.Y.E. is attractive because it is free from (*110*)
income tax, and while no method of saving is completely (*120*)
painless, if it is based on the idea of what (*130*)
you never have you never miss, it becomes less so. (*140*)
If in adverse circumstances, you are unable to keep up (*150*)
with the payments, arrangements can be made to terminate
[the (*160*)
S.A.Y.E. agreement. (*165*)

11 Business Groupings

...U.(9..ſ. at your earliest convenience

...6.ˑ..... or *...6.ᵞ........* best attention

........ᵞₕ... change of address

─ρ.ᵓ........ despatch department

..ↀ...ᵞ...... immediate attention

.....ᵝ.↲.... in reply to your letter

..........(.... large number of

.... matter of contract

...⌒↗ℂ.... mortgage account

.............ℂ out of stock

...↟......... or *.....↟.⌒ℷ..* prompt attention

...⤳ᵝₖ.... regret to inform you

....ℐ.∕ℐ.° sincere apologies

.ρᶜ......... subject to contract

.....ᵇ.∀/... take this opportunity

.........ℐ.... thank you for your letter

.....ₕ᷿...... unable to obtain

...⤳∕°...... we are sorry

.....⤳∕...... we have placed

.⤳⤳ℓ∕.... we have received your letter

.....⤳∕.⤳.. we have pleasure

⤳⤳∕°...... we were sorry

Exercises

1 Dear Sir,

    Thank you for your order which we have (10)
received today for one dozen rose bushes. These will be (20)
dispatched to you by rail, as soon as possible, and (30)
should be delivered to you before the end of the (40)
month.

    We enclose our new price-list, which operates from (50)
1st November. You can rely on our prompt attention at (60)
all times.

    Yours faithfully. (64)

2 Dear Madam,

 Many thanks for your order which will shortly   *(10)*
be receiving the attention of our dispatch department.
 The delivery   *(20)*
period is normally fourteen days, but we would appreciate
                [your *(30)*
indulgence should this period be exceeded. Our recent offers
                [have *(40)*
produced a large number of replies which we are handling   *(50)*
in strict date order.
 Please be assured of our best   *(60)*
attention at all times.
 Yours faithfully.   *(66)*

3 Dear Mrs Ledgard,

 Thank you for your letter of 2nd   *(10)*
February concerning your Rosebud Ware Cake server.
 We were sorry   *(20)*
to hear that the handle of your cake server has   *(30)*
been accidentally broken. Unfortunately, these items are not
            [now obtainable *(40)*
and we are unable to supply you with a replacement.   *(50)*
We are very sorry that we are unable to be   *(60)*
of further help to you on this occasion.
 Yours faithfully.   *(70)*

4 Dear Miss Manners,

 I am writing to express the sincere   *(10)*
thanks of the Association for a stimulating talk on 16th   *(20)*
April. It certainly ended this year's programme on a very   *(30)*
high note. You had obviously gone to a great deal   *(40)*
of trouble in preparing a lecture in which everyone present   *(50)*
was able to participate.
 Once again, many thanks for giving   *(60)*
up your valuable time to come and speak to us.   *(70)*
 Yours sincerely.   *(72)*

5 Dear Mr Thomson,

 I thank you for your letter of   *(10)*
8th October enclosing a change of address card, and I   *(20)*
note your remarks concerning the closed accounts. The
           [Standing Order *(30)*

Form for your mortgage account has been forwarded to the *(40)*
National Giro Centre for their attention.
Your investment passbook is *(50)*
returned, duly written up to date.
I hope you are *(60)*
settling into your new property and that you are all *(70)*
keeping well.
Yours sincerely. *(74)*

6 Dear Mr Sanders,
We have pleasure in advising you that, *(10)*
subject to contract, we have arranged the sale of your *(20)*
house to Mr Kenneth Spiller at an agreed price of *(30)*
thirty-five thousand pounds.
A deposit has been paid to *(40)*
us and we have today written to your solicitors asking *(50)*
them to proceed in the matter of contract.
We trust *(60)*
that the sale will proceed to completion in the normal *(70)*
way and we should like to take this opportunity of *(80)*
thanking you for your instructions in this matter.
Yours sincerely. *(90)*

7 Dear Customer,
Thank you for your application for our recent *(10)*
special offer for linen tea towels.
We are sorry to *(20)*
advise you that this item is temporarily out of stock, *(30)*
owing to overwhelmingly high demand.
We have placed an order *(40)*
for more tea towels with our supplier in Northern Ireland *(50)*
but it will take about four weeks to fulfil your *(60)*
order and we will then dispatch it as soon as *(70)*
possible.
Please accept our sincere apologies for this unfortunate
[delay *(80)*
but we are certain that you will be pleased with *(90)*
your tea towels when you receive them.
Thank you once *(100)*
again for your application.
Yours sincerely. *(106)*

8 No shorthand typist in a business office will get far (10)
without the ability to take down letters which begin: 'Thank (20)
you for your letter' or 'in reply to your letter (30)
of' or 'We have received your letter of'. Matters used (40)
to be given 'immediate attention' or dealt with 'as soon (50)
as possible' but nowadays, it may take a long time (60)
for a customer to receive a reply and he may (70)
then be told that 'because of the increased cost of (80)
raw materials, we regret to inform you that there has (90)
been a further increase in prices' or 'we are unable (100)
to obtain supplies of the goods you require'.

Some goods (110)
will be sent C.O.D., sometimes the customer will (120)
be asked to send a postal order or cheque with (130)
the order, but there will be occasions on which he (140)
has to be reminded that 'payment is overdue' and he (150)
will then be requested to 'deal with the matter at (160)
your earliest convenience'.

In this case, the letter may begin (170)
with 'Sir' instead of 'Dear Sir' and end with 'Yours (180)
truly' instead of 'Yours faithfully'.

Most firms have their own (190)
styles not only in the kind of stationery they use (200)
but also in the way the letter is worded and (210)
set out. This is known as the 'house style' of (220)
the firm. (222)

12 Company Report Groupings

.... Annual General Meeting

.... (A.G.M.)

.... Annual Return

.... annual review

.... balance sheet

.... board of directors

.... *or* .... circulated statement

.... directors' report

.... during the year under review

.... *or* .... final dividend

.... history of the company

.... heavy expenditure

.... increased profits

.... interim dividend

.... in the course of his speech

.... ladies and gentlemen

.... limited companies

.... limited liability

.... issued capital of the company

.... ordinary shares

.... preference shares

.... plant and machinery

.... report and accounts

.... Registrar of Companies

.... subsidiary companies

.... statement of accounts

.... surplus profits

.... the Chairman said

.... the following is an extract (from)

Exercises

1 Ladies and Gentlemen,
    It is my pleasant duty as Chairman (10)
of your Board to tell you that your profits today (20)
are higher than they have ever been in the history (30)
of the company. In spite of heavy expenditure on plant (40)
and machinery, we can still declare a final dividend which (50)
is better than last year's. Overseas trade has increased
                                [considerably, (60)
particularly in the United States of America, and we can (70)
look forward to even greater expansion of trade in the (80)
future. (81)

2 In the course of his speech, the Chairman said: From (10)
the directors' report, you will see that the item 'first (20)
mortgage debenture stock' has been redeemed out of surplus
                                [profits. (30)
This is in addition to the payment of an interim (40)
dividend on ordinary shares of 12½ per (50)
cent, and on preference shares of 6 per cent, less (60)
tax. I hope you will agree that the statement of (70)
accounts can be taken as read. Increased profits have been (80)
achieved in spite of technical difficulties in distribution
                                [methods during (90)
the past year. (93)

3 The Chairman, presiding at the Annual General Meeting,
                                [pointed out (10)
that during the year under review, the issued capital of (20)
the company had dropped by one hundred thousand pounds.
                                [All (30)
over the world, the cost of raw materials had risen (40)
and there was a shortage of capital for industrial development. (50)
The outlook for British industry was bleak, and was not (60)
helped by the unofficial strikes which had been affecting some (70)
of their subsidiary companies during the past months. The
                                [Board (80)
of Directors was unable to recommend payment of a dividend (90)
until increased profits were reported. (95)

53

4 Limited companies are those in which the members or

[directors *(10)*

have only limited liability for any debts which the company *(20)*
may incur. Such a company may be public or private, *(30)*
but in either case, those concerned with it must by *(40)*
law prepare two documents – the Memorandum of

[Association and the *(50)*

Articles of Association, and these must be sent to the *(60)*
Registrar of Companies at Companies House. Only when

[these have *(70)*

been accepted can the company be said to be in *(80)*
existence.

Once a year, there must be an Annual General *(90)*
Meeting of the directors in the case of a private *(100)*
company, or the shareholders and directors in the case of *(110)*
a public company. Here, the Directors' Report and the

[Statement *(120)*

of Accounts for the previous year will be presented to *(130)*
the members for acceptance. In order to save time at *(140)*
the meeting, copies of the Balance Sheet and Directors'

[Report *(150)*

are circulated beforehand and, after any discussion, they

[will be *(160)*

approved by a show of hands and 'taken as read'. *(170)*

Following the A.G.M., a copy of the Report *(180)*
and Accounts must be sent to the Registrar of Companies, *(190)*
together with an Annual Return Form, showing any changes

[in *(200)*

the shares of the company, the number of directors, the *(210)*
capital of the company, and so on. This is a *(220)*
legal requirement, and failure to comply with it may have *(230)*
serious consequences, not only for the directors, but for the *(240)*
company itself. *(242)*

13 Insurance Groupings

.... insurance companies   .... car insurance

..... some forms of   .... fire insurance
            insurance

... marine insurance   ... National Insurance

... *or* .... Lloyd's   ...... insurance policy
            of London

... no-claims bonus   .... third-party insurance

... under-insured   ... comprehensive policy

Exercises

1 Lloyd's of London is a famous insurance company and its   *(10)*
  underwriters handle marine insurance from countries all
                                        [over the world.   *(20)*
  The first fire insurance company was formed in the
                                        [seventeenth   *(30)*
  century, after the Great Fire of London. In those days,   *(40)*
  there were no local fire brigades, so the insurance companies   *(50)*
  employed their own.   *(53)*

2 Some forms of insurance, such as car insurance and insurance   *(10)*
  on houses being bought through building societies, are
                                        [compulsory. Some   *(20)*
  car-owners take out only the minimum legal requirement of   *(30)*
  third-party insurance but it may be wiser to pay   *(40)*
  more for a comprehensive policy. Other forms of insurance,
                                                [like   *(50)*
  life insurance, are optional. National Insurance
                                        [contributions are paid by   *(60)*
  most workers towards their retirement pensions.   *(66)*

3 Although an accident in a car might not be the   *(10)*
  driver's fault, his no-claims bonus will be lost or   *(20)*

55

reduced if he makes a claim against his insurance, and (*30*)
its cost cannot be recovered from the other party involved. (*40*)
If the no-claims bonus is to be preserved, the (*50*)
driver must either meet the full cost of the repair (*60*)
himself or take the other party to court. Many motorists (*70*)
are reluctant to become involved in court procedure because
[not (*80*)
only can it be a very costly business, but also (*90*)
the outcome is frequently most unsatisfactory. (*96*)

4 It is surprising how many people have their homes under- (*10*)
insured. They buy a house and insure it at the (*20*)
time of purchase, but they do not increase the premiums (*30*)
as the market value of the property increases. Neither do (*40*)
they think of raising the premiums on the house contents (*50*)
to keep pace with increasing prices, so that if these (*60*)
have to be replaced, following a fire or a burglary, (*70*)
they find that the insurance policy does not cover the (*80*)
cost of replacement. Nowadays, many insurance companies
[send information about (*90*)
this with the annual reminder that payment is due. (*99*)

5 Dear Student,
    Now you are leaving home for university, we (*10*)
wish to draw your attention to our students' insurance scheme. (*20*)
This is tailor-made to cover your personal possessions and (*30*)
includes such items as cameras, radios and hi-fi equipment. (*40*)
This policy gives cover against fire and theft while at (*50*)
college, at home during vacations, in transit and for travel (*60*)
in Europe. An ordinary household policy will not give you (*70*)
cover while living in shared accommodation as our student
[policy (*80*)
will. We, therefore, suggest that you study the enclosed
[premiums (*90*)
scale, and invite you to apply for a quotation.
    Yours (*100*)
faithfully. (*101*)

14 Banking Groupings

...... or ...... balance .... banker's order
of credit

.... credit card   .... current account

.... deposit account   .... hire purchase

.... hire-purchase   .... hospital insurance
payments

.... index-linked   .... joint-stock banks

.... National Savings   .... overdrafts
Certificates

.... rate of exchange   .... rate of interest

.... travellers' cheques .... tax-free

Exercises

1 Bank charges are not usually payable on current accounts if   (*10*)
  the account is kept in credit to the tune of   (*20*)
  one hundred pounds or above. Cheques, cheque cards, credit
  [and   (*30*)
  debit transactions are available without charges being levied,
  [provided this   (*40*)
  is done. If the balance of credit falls below this   (*50*)
  sum, bank charges are calculated on a day-to-day   (*60*)
  basis.   (*61*)

2 Overdrafts are often granted by the bank manager as a   (*10*)
  form of loan which has to be repaid within a   (*20*)
  specified period of time. Interest payable on a bank overdraft   (*30*)
  is higher than on a normal bank loan, but it   (*40*)
  is only charged on the sum actually owed, unlike some   (*50*)
  other forms of borrowing where the full interest rates
  [continue   (*60*)

to be charged until the total amount owing has been   *(70)*
repaid.   *(71)*

3 Latest government statistics show that about 60 per cent of   *(10)*
the working population in Britain now receive their pay
                       [either   *(20)*
by cheque or by having it paid into their current   *(30)*
accounts. This relieves both employers and employees from
                   [the necessity   *(40)*
of handling and carrying cash. It is also an easy   *(50)*
matter to transfer any essential savings from current account
                               [to   *(60)*
deposit account in order that they may earn some interest   *(70)*
before they are withdrawn.   *(74)*

4 A banker's order is a useful method of dealing with   *(10)*
regular payments, as not only does it ensure that the   *(20)*
payments are made on time (for example, hire-purchase
                       [payments)   *(30)*
but it is also a safeguard against forgetting to pay.   *(40)*
For instance, I am a member of a motoring organization   *(50)*
and my subscription is due in June each year. I   *(60)*
also pay a hospital insurance once a year in January.   *(70)*
I am sure that I should forget to pay these   *(80)*
at the right times, were it not for the banker's   *(90)*
orders but, as it is, I can forget about them   *(100)*
and know that all is still well.   *(107)*

5 When travelling abroad one can take money in the form   *(10)*
of either local currency or travellers' cheques, which are
                       [bought   *(20)*
before departure. It is advisable to take only enough cash   *(30)*
to cover one's immediate needs on arrival; indeed some
                       [countries   *(40)*
will, by law, allow only a very limited amount of   *(50)*
actual currency to be taken in.
     Travellers' cheques are by   *(60)*
far safer and if these are cashed at a bank   *(70)*
rather than at a shop or hotel, a better rate   *(80)*
of exchange will be given.
     It is essential to make   *(90)*

sure that the cheques are signed upon receipt so that　(*100*)
a refund can be claimed if they are accidentally lost　(*110*)
or stolen.　(*112*)

6 Those who wish to save have various methods from which　(*10*)
to choose, but one thing to consider is whether or　(*20*)
not they may need to draw out the money at　(*30*)
short notice. If not, then it is a good plan　(*40*)
to buy National Savings Certificates, as these carry a high　(*50*)
rate of interest which is tax-free. Provided they can　(*60*)
be left alone for the length of time required, they　(*70*)
represent one of the best investments for the small saver.　(*80*)
For those over retirement age, index-linked savings are
[recommended.　(*90*)
Another good long-term investment is to put money into　(*100*)
a building society. This is particularly useful for young
[people　(*110*)
who are saving up to buy their own home. The　(*120*)
Post Office savings bank is a convenient place in which　(*130*)
to keep money, as it is possible to draw it　(*140*)
out on demand at any post office in the country.　(*150*)
This saves people from having to carry too much cash　(*160*)
around when travelling. Most of the banks have credit card　(*170*)
schemes which make it easy for their customers to draw　(*180*)
out money from other banks both at home and abroad.　(*190*)
The credit card also allows people to obtain goods and　(*200*)
services without handing over actual cash at the time of　(*210*)
purchase. I wonder if the day will soon come when　(*220*)
money as we know it today is no longer necessary.　(*230*)

15 Legal Groupings

.... *or* .... Application and Affidavit

.... Court of Protection .... Deed of Severance

.... Engrossment of the .... Health Service
      Conveyance   Ombudsman

.... H.M. Land Registry .... High Court

.... High Court of Justice .... legal aid certificate

.... land certificate .... legal requirements

.... Letters of .... local authority
      Administration

.... next of kin .... Power of Attorney

.... pro rata .... Probate Court

Exercises

1 Dear Sirs,
    In the matter of Robshaw from Garside, we   *(10)*
enclose the Agreement duly signed by our clients and also   *(20)*
the Engrossment of the Conveyance which now requires
                                         [signature by *(30)*
your clients.
    Yours faithfully.   *(34)*

2 Dear Mrs Walker,
    We confirm that we have received a   *(10)*
copy of the legal aid certificate which has been issued   *(20)*
to you to help you in taking court proceedings in   *(30)*
respect of maintenance for yourself and your family.
    We have   *(40)*
today sent the papers to a barrister who will then   *(50)*
prepare your Application and Affidavit.

As soon as these come (60)
to hand, we will be in touch again.
Yours sincerely. (70)

3 Dear Mr and Mrs MacDonald,
   I am pleased to inform (10)
you that I have now received your land certificate from (20)
H.M. Land Registry, the registration of your Deed of (30)
Severance having been completed.
   Accordingly, I enclose herewith my firm's (40)
account in respect of that matter and in connection with (50)
the preparation of your wills.
   I trust the account meets (60)
with your approval and look forward to receiving settlement
                                                    [in (70)
due course.
   Yours sincerely. (74)

4 Dear Mr Blackburn,
   We enclose a copy of a letter (10)
which we have today received from your wife's solicitors.
   It (20)
does not appear from the contents that she has made (30)
any application for passports or made any other arrangements
                                                    [to (40)
take your two children to her parents' address in Canada. (50)
On your behalf I telephoned your wife's solicitors this
                                              [morning (60)
and asked them to let me have any further details (70)
regarding her circumstances and whereabouts as soon as
                                          [they have (80)
any further information.
   Yours sincerely. (85)

5 A Power of Attorney may sound like something from a (10)
television programme, but it is a very old form of (20)
English law.
   Anyone can use a Power of Attorney to (30)
give a nominee authority to act on financial matters so (40)
long as the nominee is willing to act.
   It may (50)

be for a short time as when a legal document (60)
needs to be signed and the person concerned is temporarily (70)
living abroad; or a more permanent arrangement when
[serious illness (80)
or old age prevents a person from being able to (90)
manage his own financial affairs. In this case a Court (100)
of Protection grants a suitable person Power of Attorney
[and (110)
ensures that he always acts in the best interests of (120)
the person he represents. (124)

6 The word 'Ombudsman' comes from Sweden and means
['a grievance (10)
man'. The post has fairly recently been revived in Britain (20)
and an Ombudsman is appointed as a watch dog to (30)
assess the state's involvement in people's lives. There are
[three (40)
types – the Health Service Ombudsman, the Parliamentary
[Ombudsman and the (50)
Local Authority Ombudsman.
   If a person believes he has been (60)
unfairly treated by, say, the Local Planning Department, or
[the (70)
Area Health Authority, he has the right to appeal to (80)
the relevant Ombudsman who will investigate on his behalf
[and (90)
deal with complaints of alleged bad administration.
   The Parliamentary Ombudsman (100)
can be contacted only by an M.P. on a (110)
constituent's behalf, but the other two may be contacted
[direct. (120)
If a person disagrees with a decision made by a (130)
government department it does not automatically follow
[that the Ombudsman (140)
will act for that person. The Ombudsman must be satisfied (150)
that a genuine grievance exists before taking up the case. (160)

7 If a person dies without leaving a will, he is (10)
said to be Intestate and his next of kin must (20)
apply, through a solicitor, for 'Letters of Administration'.
[This is (30)

a document issued by the High Court of Justice, through (40)
the District Probate Court, or Registry, granting the
[applicant the (50)
right to any money, property or other possessions of the (60)
deceased person. This process takes time and therefore it is (70)
a wise move for everyone to make a will at (80)
some time or other during his or her lifetime.
If (90)
changes in legacies or bequests need to be made later (100)
on, this is easily done by adding a clause called (110)
a codicil to the original will. A will must be (120)
administered by trustees and the banks, or solicitors may
[act (130)
as trustees for those who have no one else to (140)
see to their affairs, or who prefer to leave matters (150)
in the hands of a firm rather than one or (160)
two individuals. (162)

8 Dear Madam,
Re Benjamin Sykes Deceased
Under the will of (10)
the above-named, your late mother, Mrs Lucy Clarkson, was (20)
bequeathed a legacy of five hundred pounds. We are informed (30)
by her brother, Mr H. Sykes, that you are the (40)
only child and sole beneficiary of her estate and therefore (50)
entitled to this legacy.
Following the death of the life (60)
tenant, Miss M. E. Sykes, in April of this year (70)
we are now in a position to distribute this estate. (80)
Unfortunately, the investment has failed to realize sufficient
[capital to (90)
satisfy all the legatees as the trustees invested the money (100)
in 1947 in 3 per cent War Stock (110)
which now stands at less than half the price they (120)
paid for it.
Consequently, all legacies in this estate have (130)
abated 'pro rata' and I now enclose herein our cheque (140)
for three hundred pounds in satisfaction of your legacy and (150)
we shall be obliged if you will kindly acknowledge its (160)
receipt.
Yours faithfully. (163)

16 Technological Groupings

ATOMIC

..........ᴄ..........

.........ᴄ.ᴴ.... atomic energy   ....ᴄ.ᴏ.ᐩ.... atomic bomb

.........ᴄ.ᐟ.... atomic pile   ....ᴄ.ᒧ...... atomic power

.........ᴄℓ...... atomic fuel   ....ᴄ.ᴊ...... atomic waste

ELECTRONIC/S

..ᴋᴄ....ᴋᴄ..   ..ᴋᴄ.ᴊ..... electronic typewriter

..ᴋᴄ.ᴴ....... electronics engineer   ...ᴋᴄ.ᴊ...... electronic stencil

ELECTRO

......ᴌ........

..ᴌ.ᴄᴊ.... electromagnet   .ᴌ.ᴊᴄ...... electro-graphics

MICRO

.....ᴄᴄ......

.ᴄᴄ.ᴄ..... micro-computer   .ᴄᴄ.ᴊ...... microchip

...ᴄᴄᴊᴩ.... microphone   ...ᴄᴄ.ᴧ... microwave

.....ᴄᴄ.ᴊᴄ.. micro-graphics

TECHNICAL

....ᴄ....
....

.........ᴄᴊ..... technical college   ....ᴄᴧ.... technical ability

TECHNOLOGICAL

........T........
........⌐T⌐........ technological
       revolution

........Tϛ........ technological skills

........Tꭓ........ technological age

VIDEO

.....V⌐.......

...V⌐ᴑ..... video cassette

.V......ᴢ..... video recorder

...V⌐eꞇ... video screen

...V⌐e..... video disk

...V⌐ᴦ...... video tape

....V⌐ᴣ..... videogram

Exercises

1 One of the parish councillors who was by profession an   (*10*)
electronics engineer, offered to install a microphone system
                                   [to improve (*20*)
the acoustics of the village hall.   (*26*)

2 Many technical colleges today find that, in order to equip   (*10*)
students to meet the demands of this technological age, less   (*20*)
time can be allocated to learning shorthand than in the   (*30*)
past.   (*31*)

3 A Royal Commission, carrying out an investigation into
                                    [the disposal (*10*)
of atomic waste, said it was absolutely necessary that those   (*20*)
responsible could give an undertaking to the general public
                                        [that (*30*)
there was no long-term danger involved.   (*37*)

4 The development of the microchip has caused a
                         [technological revolution (*10*)
in the developed countries, so universities and technical
                                 [colleges are (*20*)
having to provide courses to train students in the new   (*30*)

technological skills. Many of today's students will expect
[eventually to *(40)*
become computer programmers, word-processing operators
[and electronics engineers. *(49)*

5 There is no doubt that the technological revolution has
[swept *(10)*
the world with a vengeance since the end of the *(20)*
Second World War. Although the horrendous implications
[of the dropping *(30)*
of the first atomic bomb were not realized, atomic energy *(40)*
has since been used to benefit humankind rather than to *(50)*
destroy it. *(52)*

17 Technical Terms

.... astronaut   .... cosmonaut

.... Ceefax   .... data base

.... data processing   .... floppy disk

.... hi-tech   .... lasar beams

.... peripherals   .... Prestel

.... silicone chip   .... Teletext

.... vinyl   .... view data

Exercises

1 In 1969 the first astronauts landed on the   *(10)*
  moon and despite the poor quality of the television pictures *(20)*
  it was a very thrilling moment. The astronauts brought back   *(30)*
  many rock and soil samples for analysis but the moon   *(40)*
  still remains as much of a mystery as it ever   *(50)*
  was. The experts are now turning their attention to more   *(60)*
  distant planets and cosmonauts are being trained with a view *(70)*
  to making landings elsewhere in the solar system.   *(78)*

2 A late twentieth-century revolution in cooking has arrived
                                              [with *(10)*
  the introduction of the microwave oven, which cooks faster
                                              [than *(20)*
  any other method. The microwaves, which are similar to
                                              [radio *(30)*
  waves, bombard the food inside the oven and cause the   *(40)*
  molecules within the food to vibrate and generate heat. It   *(50)*
  is a very speedy process which helps to retain the   *(60)*
  flavour and preserve the vitamin content of the food. Because *(70)*
  cooking time is so short, the oven uses far less   *(80)*
  electricity than more conventional types of cooking.   *(87)*

3 A Cash Dispenser Card and its Personal Identification
[Number should   *(10)*
always be kept separately because the card is useless to   *(20)*
a thief without the PIN number. Should the C.D.   *(30)*
card and the PIN number be lost at the same   *(40)*
time, a would-be thief can withdraw the maximum permitted   *(50)*
amount in any one day from the machine. Not many   *(60)*
people are aware that the card-holder is responsible for   *(70)*
the loss of the money, because one of the conditions   *(80)*
of issue is that the PIN number should be kept   *(90)*
secret.   *(91)*

4 Word Processing is concerned with the production of all
[types   *(10)*
of documents.
  1 Preparation, usually by means of a keyboard   *(20)*
on to a Visual Display Unit.
  2 Filing on to   *(30)*
a floppy disk which holds between twenty-five to one   *(40)*
hundred A4 sheets depending on size and whether they   *(50)*
are single or double-sided.
  3 Instant retrieval by recalling   *(60)*
to V.D.U. and then by printing either from   *(70)*
V.D.U. or direct from file.
  4 Editing in   *(80)*
the form of making amendments such as moving the text,   *(90)*
insertion and deletion.   *(93)*

5 One of the complaints about the change-over to Word   *(10)*
Processing is that of eye-strain as a result of   *(20)*
working at the V.D.U. Because most offices are   *(30)*
well lit, often with strip lighting, it makes conditions
[difficult   *(40)*
for someone using a screen where lower than normal lighting   *(50)*
levels are required to offset the possibility of glare.
Most   *(60)*
eye-strain results because the eyes have to make continual   *(70)*
adjustments to the contrast between the brightness of the
[screen   *(80)*
and the general illumination of the office. This results in   *(90)*

fatigue and lowers the ability to concentrate and although
[there (*100*)
are various gadgets available which are said to solve the (*110*)
problem, they do not always help. (*116*)

6 Prestel is a computer-based view data service offered on (*10*)
hire by the Post Office. The equipment involved is either (*20*)
a special Prestel television or an adaptor which is fitted (*30*)
to an existing T.V. and then connected to the (*40*)
telephone. A small keyboard is also necessary to contact the (*50*)
Prestel computer through the telephone line.
A directory is supplied (*60*)
free of charge every three months listing Prestel subscribers
[and (*70*)
their numbers. Much of the information is provided by
[well- (*80*)
known organizations, and the store of information numbers
[over two (*90*)
hundred thousand pages, which are constantly updated.
Types of information (*100*)
available include financial statistics, Stock Exchange
|share prices, commercial and (*110*)
industrial news, guides to the theatre and tourism. (*118*)

7 It is a far cry from the days twenty years (*10*)
ago when a computer filled a room, to the portable (*20*)
machines now on sale which weigh under 10 kilogrammes
[and (*30*)
which are compact enough to take on an air liner (*40*)
as hand baggage.
Even though the machines are small, most (*50*)
of them are powerful 16K machines with non-glare (*60*)
screens, large capacity memories and either one or two dual- (*70*)
sided floppy disks which give instantly accessible information.
Keyboards are (*80*)
detachable and can be used over a metre away from (*90*)
the computer. It is possible to buy extra accessories such (*100*)
as a composite video which could connect to an external (*110*)
monitor and also a time and data clock. (*118*)

8 The home computer is one of the smaller range of   *(10)*
micro–computers, or micros, and these are in demand both   *(20)*
for educational purposes and for personal amusement. Like
                                      [any other   *(30)*
computer it consists of three different parts. Firstly an input   *(40)*
mechanism, generally like a typewriter keyboard, although
                                [some types work   *(50)*
by means of light pressure on apparently static pads.
                                          [Secondly,   *(60)*
the computer itself – the C.P.U. or Central Processing   *(70)*
Unit, together with a memory or storage unit known as   *(80)*
RAM, or Random Access Memory, which is measured
                                      [according to   *(90)*
how much information it can store. Thirdly, output is
                                           [given   *(100)*
from an ordinary T.V. screen, although the more
                                  [sophisticated   *(110)*
type of home computer has its own screen or V.   *(120)*
D.U.   *(122)*

9 Much has been said about the paperless office, but not   *(10)*
much has been said about the type of furniture which   *(20)*
will be used in it. Present–day office furniture is   *(30)*
not made of wood but has a simulated oak or   *(40)*
other natural wood finish made of vinyl foil. These vinyl   *(50)*
veneers are easy to clean and less easily damaged than   *(60)*
wood. The new type of furniture comes in a variety   *(70)*
of permutations which include not only single and double
                                      [pedestal   *(80)*
desks incorporating various types of drawers and cupboards,
                                      [but also   *(90)*
conference and occasional tables for the reception area.
  Matching metal   *(100)*
filing cabinets complete the office transformation, and as
                                      [the vinyl   *(110)*
coating is also scratch and stain-resistant, it ensures a   *(120)*
smart-looking office for some considerable time.   *(127)*

10 Laser beams, a hi-tech twentieth-century discovery, are
                                        [used   *(10)*
in industry, for bar codes in supermarkets, in surgery and   *(20)*

are now being used in beauty treatments. It is claimed (30)
that the use of lasers in beauty salons will soon (40)
be as common as the sun bed.
The word 'laser' (50)
stands for Light Amplification by Stimulated Emission of
[Radiation, or (60)
in simpler terms, concentrated light.
Beauty therapists are now being (70)
trained to use the laser in the form of a (80)
metal pencil for acne scars, face lifts, removal of tattoos (90)
and other cosmetic problems. It is said to be quite (100)
painless, although several treatments may be necessary for
[long-lasting (110)
effects. But the laser could be dangerous in unqualified
[hands (120)
and should be treated with great respect as the long- (130)
term effects of laser therapy are not yet understood. (139)

11 Modern technology has helped to make direct mail
[advertising an (10)
increasingly successful method of selling. Agencies exist
[which, on payment (20)
of a fee, supply computerized lists of names and addresses, (30)
thus enabling letters to be sent to potential customers. Bulk (40)
printing can be arranged reasonably cheaply using laser
[printing methods (50)
which give the impression and prestige of an individually
[typed (60)
letter.
Firms who adopt this system claim a high success (70)
rate and it is possible to evaluate its success by (80)
the number of replies received.
Against this, one has to (90)
balance the cost of postage, including a reply envelope and (100)
any leaflets enclosed. There is bound to be considerable
[wastage (110)
because the rate of response is usually an unknown factor. (120)
Nevertheless, this form of advertising is growing rapidly
[and total (130)
sales in the U.K. are said to be worth (140)
about three million pounds a year. (146)

18 Press and Political Groupings

...... *X* ..... accident black spots

.... *Cᵧ* .... assaulting a police officer

...... *ʰ* .... at the end of the day

... *ℓⁿ* ...... bound over in the sum of

... *ℚ* .... breaking and entering

.... *ℚ* .. breach of the peace

... *ℬ* ...... before the court

.... *Cᵧ* ...... cause of the accident

...... *ᑫⁿ* ... charged with

...... *ℓᵒ* ..... conditional discharge

...... *ℓᵈ* .... Counsel for the Defence

..... *Xⁿ* .... cross-examination

...... *ℓᵖ* ... Counsel for the Prosecution

— *ᵖ* —ᵥᵧ dangerous driving

—ᵒ —ᵧᵧ.. disqualified from driving

— *ᵏ* —ᵥ.. drink and drive

— *ᵏ* —ᵥᵧ drinking and driving

— *ᵛᵗ* .. driving without a licence

— *ᵛᵗ* ʸ driving without due care and attention

... *ᵥᵒᵗ* .... evidence was given

... *ᵍᵗᶜ* ... first offence

.... *ℓ* ...... from evidence received

.. *ℓᵗᵇ* .... freedom of the Press

..... *ᵖℚℓ* ... grievous bodily harm

.. *ℚᵗ* .... last but not least

ℚᵐᵧᵒ ..... last but by no means least

... *ℓᵗ* ...... national interest

ᵒ —ᵗᵒ⁻ⁿ ordered to make restitution

72

...*(shorthand)*. plead guilty   ...*(shorthand)*. pleaded guilty

...*(shorthand)*...... taken into custody

...*(shorthand)*..... at this point in time   ...*(shorthand)*..... balance of payments

...*(shorthand)*......... Chancellor of the   ...*(shorthand)*.... deeper and deeper
          Exchequer

...*(shorthand)*..... economic policy   ...*(shorthand)*... European Economic
                                        Community

(...*(shorthand)*.... E.E.C.)   ...*(shorthand)*.. from the grass roots

...*(shorthand)*.... generally speaking

...*(shorthand)*.. House of Lords   ...*(shorthand)*.... in all probability

...*(shorthand)*... international trade   ...*(shorthand)*...... in this day and age

...*(shorthand)*... Leader of the   ...*(shorthand)*.... National Health
          Opposition   Service

...*(shorthand)*.... political parties   ...*(shorthand)*.... political party
                                    conferences

...*(shorthand)*.... Prime Minister   ...*(shorthand)*...... value added tax

                            (...*(shorthand)*....... V.A.T.)

Distinguishing outlines

...*(shorthand)*... exhorted   ...*(shorthand)*..... exerted

Exercises

1 The freedom of the Press and the freedom of the   (*10*)
  individual are matters about which we hear a great deal   (*20*)
  in this country, or, I suppose, in any democratically run   (*30*)
  society. It is sometimes in the national interest to curb   (*40*)
  these two freedoms, but whenever this happens there is an   (*50*)

outcry from the general public who, generally speaking, do
[not *(60)*
take kindly to having their freedom curtailed. *(67)*

2 Before the court were two youths charged with dangerous
[driving *(10)*
and driving without a licence or a certificate of insurance. *(20)*
As it was his first offence, the younger one was *(30)*
bound over in the sum of fifty pounds and given *(40)*
a conditional discharge. The older one was placed on
[probation *(50)*
for a period of twelve months. Evidence was given that *(60)*
the car involved had been stolen and the youths were *(70)*
ordered to make restitution to the owner in the sum *(80)*
of one hundred pounds for inconvenience caused. *(87)*

3 Under cross-examination, the prisoner admitted assaulting
[a police officer *(10)*
while being taken into custody for committing a breach of *(20)*
the peace. The assault took place on the way to *(30)*
the police station. From evidence received, the man
[appeared to *(40)*
have a history of violence, which began when he was *(50)*
sent to an approved school in his teens, for breaking *(60)*
and entering. Since then, he had developed an extremely anti- *(70)*
social attitude and on several occasions had attacked
[members of *(80)*
the public towards whom he felt antagonistic. The case was *(90)*
adjourned until further witnesses could be called. *(97)*

4 Day after day and month after month, the courts are *(10)*
full of people who have been charged with various driving *(20)*
offences. Some will be disqualified from driving, some will
[plead *(30)*
guilty to driving without a licence, and others will be *(40)*
convicted of dangerous driving.
   Advertising campaigns for accident prevention do *(50)*
little to reduce the number of motorists who drink and *(60)*
drive, although it has been stated that a large number *(70)*
of accidents result from drinking and driving and many more *(80)*
are caused through driving without due care and attention in *(90)*

74

accident black spots.

There are many cases where speeding in (*100*)
fog has been the cause of the accident and lately (*110*)
it has been pointed out that people who have to (*120*)
take certain drugs should, in all probability, not be driving (*130*)
at all. The car is a lethal weapon, but many (*140*)
people still handle it with less care than they would (*150*)
handle a gun. (*153*)

5 Shorthand writers need to have as wide a knowledge of (*10*)
words as possible, although naturally, they will find certain
[jobs (*20*)
lead them to make use of a specialized vocabulary. For (*30*)
example, if they are asked to report a meeting at (*40*)
which there is a speaker, they may need such phrases (*50*)
as 'the Chairman said', 'in the course of his speech' (*60*)
and 'last, but not least' or 'last, but by no (*70*)
means least', as well as 'in conclusion', 'Ladies and
[Gentlemen' (*80*)
and 'Mr Chairman' or 'Madam Chairman'. At the end of (*90*)
the meeting someone is sure to propose a vote of (*100*)
thanks to the speaker.

A court reporter, on the other (*110*)
hand, may need to write phrases like 'breach of the (*120*)
peace', 'grievous bodily harm', 'assaulting a police officer'
[and 'conditional (*130*)
discharge'. During a hearing, Counsel for the Prosecution
[or Counsel (*140*)
for the Defence may cross-examine the witnesses. A case (*150*)
may be heard in the High Court or referred to (*160*)
a Court of Appeal.

If a shorthand writer does not (*170*)
know a quick way of writing such phrases, there is (*180*)
less chance that he or she will be able to (*190*)
take a complete or satisfactory note, so it is worth (*200*)
spending time in learning and practising any word
[groupings which (*210*)
he or she thinks may, at some time, be useful. (*220*)

6 Members of Parliament and other speakers at the several
[annual (*10*)

political party conferences give journalists and reporters
[an opportunity to (20)
put into practice their knowledge of clichés and similar well- (30)
known expressions. These will, doubtless, include 'from
[the grass roots' (40)
'in this day and age' and 'at this point in (50)
time'.

We shall be told by the Prime Minister that (60)
our balance of payments has never been better and by (70)
the Leader of the Opposition that it has never been (80)
worse. Companies will be exhorted by the Chancellor of the (90)
Exchequer to put massive investment into British industry
[in order (100)
to save firms from going out of business.

We shall (110)
be told by one side that our membership of the (120)
European Economic Community is the best economic
[policy and by (130)
the other that belonging to the E.E.C. is (140)
affecting our international trade and drawing us deeper
[and deeper (150)
into debt. There will, in all probability, be debates on (160)
the future of the National Health Service, and some
[delegate (170)
is sure to call for the abolition of the House (180)
of Lords or value added tax.

Whichever party is not (190)
in power will blame the one which is for the (200)
present state of the economy and will try to convince (210)
the rank and file members that things will be quite (220)
different if they win the next election. But, at the (230)
end of the day, when everyone has departed, the majority (240)
of the general public will forget all that has been (250)
said until the same time next year, when it will (260)
start all over again. (264)

19 Difficult Words Section

1 Words ending in -TION and -SHL

......✑.... manipulation   ....✑.... radiation

......✑........ capitation   ....✑.... legislation

......✑.... immersion   ....✑........ allocation

......✑.... deficient   ....✑..... differentiation

......✑........ rational   ....✑..... *or* ......✑..... pronunciation

......✑.... impressionable   ....✑...... controversial

......✑.... differential   ....✑..s. deferential

......✑..s.... consequential   ....✑..... superficial

Exercises

1 Much of the government's proposed legislation has caused
                           [controversial debates   *(10)*
  in Parliament.   *(12)*

2 A great deal of manipulation was required before the
                                  [immersion   *(10)*
  heater could be satisfactorily disconnected.   *(15)*

3 Pay rises acceptable to the lower-paid workers are often   *(10)*
  rejected by their better-paid colleagues who wish to preserve   *(20)*
  a differential pay system.   *(24)*

4 The allocation of funds on a capitation basis may result   *(10)*
  in educational establishments accepting more students than
                                  [can be comfortably   *(20)*
  accommodated in the building.   *(24)*

5 Differentiation between New Zealand and Australian
                         [speech is difficult for   *(10)*

Europeans. The pronunciation of words in these countries
[also has *(20)*
certain similarities with those spoken by South Africans. *(28)*

6 It is a well-known fact that many who survived *(10)*
the dropping of the atomic bomb in Japan at the *(20)*
end of the Second World War, eventually died of radiation *(30)*
sickness. *(31)*

7 It is not possible to have a rational debate with *(10)*
people who hold extreme views, as they usually pay only *(20)*
superficial attention to any reasonable argument which
[contradicts their own *(30)*
beliefs. *(31)*

8 The young are often impressionable because they are deficient
[in *(10)*
knowledge and experience. As they grow older, there is a *(20)*
consequential increase in their ability to think for
[themselves and *(30)*
not to follow blindly where others lead. *(37)*

2 Words ending in -ANCE and -ENCE

.... *or* .... countenance .... grievance

.... maintenance .... remittance

.... perseverance .... inference

.... *or* .... insolence .... prevalence

.... recurrence .... subsidence

Exercises

1 Because of the prevalence of malaria in certain countries,
[travellers *(10)*
visiting such areas are advised to take anti-malaria tablets. *(20)*

2 The youth's apparently deferential manner contradicted
[the expression on his *(10)*

face. It was clear that he was nursing a grievance (20)
against those in authority. (24)

3 Owing to subsidence, part of the house has had to (10)
be rebuilt, but it is hoped that regular maintenance and (20)
inspection will prevent a recurrence of the trouble. (28)

4 If a person is unwilling to show perseverance in achieving (10)
a skill, then the inference must be drawn that he (20)
does not really wish to become proficient in it. (29)

5 Although the term 'remittance' in business is understood
[to mean (10)
money sent in payment, in a medical context it can (20)
mean a lessening of pain and a consequent improvement of (30)
health in the case of a serious medical condition. (39)

6 It is not possible to countenance the suggestion that the (10)
Football Club should be allowed to attend the return match (20)
after the insolence shown to the referee on the last (30)
occasion, which led to the police being called on to (40)
the pitch. (42)

3 Words ending in -ABLE and -IBLE

...... hospitable   ...... despicable

...... reputable   ...... equitable

...... accessible   ...... compatible

...... eligible   ...... *or* ...... infallible

...... intelligible   ...... susceptible

Exercises

1 Most human beings are susceptible to flattery, but those
[who (10)
flatter are not necessarily the most compatible people to be (20)
with. (21)

2 Few crimes are more despicable than those carried out against   *(10)*
  old people and animals, who are unable to defend themselves   *(20)*
  against their attackers.   *(23)*

3 Since he is a senior member of a highly reputable   *(10)*
  firm of lawyers, I think he is the most eligible   *(20)*
  candidate for the chairmanship of this society.   *(27)*

4 While I agree that his speech was the most intelligible   *(10)*
  one made in the debate, he is not infallible and   *(20)*
  some of his facts were incorrect.   *(26)*

5 Those who journey to the more inaccessible regions of the   *(10)*
  world, generally confirm how hospitable they find the native
  [peoples   *(20)*
  who, by our standards, are usually extremely poor.   *(28)*

6 It should be the aim of any democratically elected
  [government   *(10)*
  to create a more equitable society, but ideas about what   *(20)*
  constitutes fairness and justice vary considerably from
  [person to person.   *(30)*

4 Words ending in -RITY and -LITY

...... posterity   ...... inferiority   ...... rarity

...... security   ...... dexterity   ...... debility

...... mobility   ...... morality   ...... fatality

...... hospitality

Exercises

1 Certain groups of disabled people are entitled to receive a   *(10)*
  mobility allowance to enable them to get about.   *(18)*

2 People who have equal dexterity with their left and right   *(10)*
  hands are something of a rarity, but when this happens,   *(20)*

they are said to be ambidextrous. (26)

3 The fatalities of war are honoured by posterity in services (10)
of remembrance, but these do not, unfortunately, prevent
[the same (20)
mistakes from being made by succeeding generations. (27)

4 It is said that individuals who are given affection and (10)
security in early childhood are better able to overcome life's (20)
difficulties than those who are neglected by their parents. (29)

5 In the Middle Ages, it was customary for morality plays (10)
to be performed on carts in the streets. As few (20)
ordinary people could then read, the plays provided religious
[instruction (30)
as well as entertainment. (34)

6 The feeling of inferiority experienced by some people may be (10)
due partly to the fact that they are suffering from (20)
general debility. In this case, if their health can be (30)
improved, they often become more confident. (36)

5 Miscellaneous difficult words

.... contemporary   .... monopolize

.... parallel   .... *or* .... coincidence

.... surreptitious   .... vehement

.... corroborate   .... annihilate

.... notwithstanding   .... uncommunicative

.... incompatible   .... unconstitutional

.... incentive   .... uncomplimentary

.... incessant   .... increment

.... disestablishmentarianism

81

Exercises

1 It was easy to see from their incessant wrangling that *(10)*
  they were a totally incompatible pair. *(16)*

2 Notwithstanding the uncomplimentary remarks made about
  [the meal by several *(10)*

  members of the family, no one refused a second helping *(20)*
  where it was offered. *(24)*

3 The rebels were forced to arrange surreptitious meetings to
  [escape *(10)*
  the attention of those who had threatened to annihilate them *(20)*
  if they were ever caught together. *(26)*

4 I am pleased to corroborate the fact that the annual *(10)*
  increment to your salary has been confirmed and the new *(20)*
  rate will be paid from next month. *(27)*

5 I found the boys in the gym, exercising on the *(10)*
  parallel bars and, holding back a vehement desire to abuse *(20)*
  them for entering without permission, I pointed out that they *(30)*
  were breaking the regulations by being there unsupervised. *(38)*

6 The committee decided that the secretary had acted in an *(10)*
  unconstitutional manner by taking it upon herself to invite Mr *(20)*
  Smith to address the meeting, as the society's rules clearly *(30)*
  stated that all speakers must be approved by the Chairman *(40)*
  before they received an official invitation. *(46)*

7 There is little incentive to talk to an uncommunicative
  [person, *(10)*
  as it is difficult to keep a conversation going by *(20)*
  oneself and hard work thinking of new things to say. *(30)*
  It is easier to be with people who monopolize the *(40)*
  conversation, as they are usually quite happy just for
  [someone *(50)*
  to listen. *(52)*

8 It was a strange coincidence that the man who came *(10)*
  to my assistance should turn out to be a contemporary *(20)*

82

of mine, as I had not seen him since we (*30*)
left college many years before and had, therefore, no idea (*40*)
that he would be travelling to the same holiday resort (*50*)
on the same plane. (*54*)

20 General Dictation Passages for Building Speed

(See the Groupings List at the end of this book and also *Teeline Word List* for reference.)

1 ....⌇.... for the government ....⌇...... government's intention ....⌇....... spokesman

A spokesman for the government said that substantial [wage increases (*10*) were out of the question at the present moment. Increased (*20*) wages, in whatever sector, led to increased prices. This had (*30*) been stressed over and over again. It was the government's (*40*) intention to reduce inflation by the end of the year. (*50*) After that, they would look into the matter of special (*60*) cases. (*61*)

2 ....⌇..... Pavilion

The Chairman proposed that the sooner a precise date could (*10*) be given when the Society would allow the workmen to (*20*) gain access to the spare ground behind the Pavilion, the (*30*) better it would be. (*30*)

The cricket season would soon be (*40*) upon us and it was vital that the new changing (*50*) rooms should be ready if the games were to be (*60*) financially successful. (*72*)

3 ....⌇.... air-conditioned ....⌇..... Morocco ....⌇....... Manchester ....⌇..... vaccination ....⌇... Tangier

Dear Sir, In response to your query, I now enclose (*10*) full details and prices of the air–coach tour to (*20*) Morocco.

The holidays are of two weeks' duration and, as   *(30)*
you will see, the flight is from Manchester to Tangier   *(40)*
where an air-conditioned coach with English-speaking
                         [hostess will *(50)*
meet you for your four-centre tour into the Atlas   *(60)*
Mountains. We strongly advise certain vaccinations for
                      [destinations outside Europe. *(70)*
Visas will not be required for British passport holders.
    Yours   *(80)*
faithfully.   *(81)*

4 .... meals a day   .... for their own

.... Third World   .... one of our

.... majority   .... standard of living

There are many parts of the world in which the   *(10)*
standard of living is so low that it is hard   *(20)*
for us in this country to imagine what it is   *(30)*
like. Most people in the United Kingdom expect to eat   *(40)*
at least three meals a day, but in some countries   *(50)*
one meal every day is all a person can hope   *(60)*
for and even this may be less than one of   *(70)*
our meals. Most people here eat too much for their   *(80)*
own good, but in the Third World the majority eat   *(90)*
too little.   *(92)*

5 .... windscreen   .... *or* .... bracket

.... laminated   .... toughened

.... collision   .... obliterating

One of the main danger areas in a car comes   *(10)*
from the accidental shattering of the windscreen, either
                        [from a *(20)*
collision or a thrown-up stone.
    The safest glass at   *(30)*
present is laminated glass which cracks into very large
                        [sections, *(40)*

thereby enabling the driver to continue driving without too

[much (*50*)

difficulty. Many cars in the lower price bracket use

[toughened (*60*)

glass only, because it is more economical to fit than (*70*)
laminated glass.

However, it is by no means as safe (*80*)
because it shatters into masses of small pieces when it (*90*)
breaks, thus completely obliterating the driver's view. (*97*)

6 .... best results .... deterred

.... *or* .... function .... aerial

A modern television set is designed and manufactured to

[high (*10*)

international standards, but care must be taken to observe

[certain (*20*)

precautions so that the best results will be obtained with (*30*)
maximum safety. It must be correctly installed and must

[have (*40*)

an adequate aerial system if it is to function properly. (*50*)
The set must not stand directly on a carpet or (*60*)
close to curtains, otherwise it may overheat and cause fire (*70*)
damage. Children should be deterred from pushing anything

[into the (*80*)

back of the casing which, at the best will affect (*90*)
performance and, at the worst, could result in an electric (*100*)
shock.

Regular maintenance by a qualified television engineer

[will keep (*110*)

the set operating efficiently. (*114*)

7 .... unobtrusive .... ultra-violet

.... identified .... unclaimed

.... post-code .... in this way

A different, but very effective use of your post-code (*10*)

is to help protect your valuables or other property from (20)
theft.

The items should be marked with your post-code (30)
in as unobtrusive a place as possible, using a security (40)
marker pen. These pens are readily available, are
[inexpensive and (50)
use invisible ink which can only be read under an (60)
ultra-violet lamp.

In this way you stand a much (70)
better chance of recovering your property if it has been (80)
lost or stolen, because it can then be identified. Strange (90)
as it may seem, much lost or stolen property is (100)
eventually recovered by the police, but remains unclaimed
[as it (110)
is not possible to trace the owner. (117)

8 .... great advantage .... English people

.... to the fact that .... nationalities

.... bilingual .... switch-over

It is a great advantage to be able to speak (10)
a foreign language, but in the past this has not (20)
been something for which English people have been noted.
[Whether (30)
this is due to laziness on our part or to (40)
the fact that most other nationalities learn our language and (50)
prefer to practise on us, rather than have us practise (60)
on them, no one has yet discovered.

However, a bilingual (70)
secretary or journalist is likely to find much more interesting (80)
work than if he or she spoke only his or (90)
her own tongue, and shorthand writers who can take
[dictation (100)
in more than one language should have no difficulty in (110)
obtaining employment. (112)

9 .... in order to have .... patio

.... open air .... pre-cast

.... concrete   .... barbecue

.... verbal   .... first place

.... telephone conversation

Dear Mr James,
    Further to our telephone conversation, I am   (*10*)
interested in having a patio built, either at the side   (*20*)
or rear of my house, in order to have a   (*30*)
dining area in the open air. Both these areas are   (*40*)
in full sun in summer for the greater part of   (*50*)
the day.
    As natural stone is now very expensive, I   (*60*)
was thinking in terms of pre-cast concrete blocks with   (*70*)
patterned paving in different colours. I would also like
                                                   [some (*80*)
provision to be made for a barbecue area.
    I can   (*90*)
be at home any evening next week and shall be   (*100*)
pleased to see you any time after 7 p.m. so   (*110*)
that you can give me a verbal estimate in the   (*120*)
first place.
    Yours sincerely.   (*124*)

10 .... *or* .... fulfilling   .... cross-section

.... random   .... surveys

.... interviewers   .... authority

.... bona fides   .... adheres

.... code of conduct   .... market research
                                            organization

Any organization which gives a service to the public or   (*10*)
supplies goods must be aware of the opinions of that   (*20*)
public in order to make sure that it is fulfilling   (*30*)
those needs. This is done by conducting interviews with a   (*40*)

cross-section of the population chosen at random. Surveys
[are (*50*)
conducted by trained interviewers either in one particular
[area or (*60*)
in several areas of the country, and people of all (*70*)
ages and from all social groups are chosen to ensure (*80*)
that a representative cross-section of opinion is obtained. (*90*)
The interviewers will carry a card of authority often with (*100*)
a photograph to ensure their bona fides and that they (*110*)
adhere to a strict code of conduct on behalf of (*120*)
the market research organization they represent. (*126*)

11 .... recommend   .... delightful

.... Adriatic   .... pedalos

.... volleyball   .... discos

.... out-of-season   .... lively

.... speciality

May we recommend to you one of our delightful holidays (*10*)
on the Adriatic Coast, especially if you have to take (*20*)
your holidays either early or late in the season.
The (*30*)
hotel is situated at the edge of a sandy beach (*40*)
where boats and pedalos can be hired. The hotel also (*50*)
has a large swimming pool with two sun terraces and (*60*)
dancing every night. There is also a sports club with (*70*)
tennis, table tennis and volleyball available at very cheap
[rates. (*80*)
In the town only a few minutes' walk away are (*90*)
many restaurants where local sea food is a speciality, several (*100*)
little taverns and lively discos.
You will be surprised at (*110*)
the low price of the package deal we can offer (*120*)
for out-of-season holidays. (*125*)

12 .... TOG   .... duvet   .... filament

..._⌐_... *or* ..._⌐_... Polyester   ....↴.... Terylene

≡_⌐_ ....↳... hygienically

Dear Madam,
    Thank you for your letter of 17th September.   *(10)*
I was interested to hear that you are thinking of   *(20)*
changing from the more traditional methods of bed
                                    [coverings to *(30)*
a duvet, but can fully appreciate your concern about
                                    [feather *(40)*
and down fillings because of your chest complaint.
    I can   *(50)*
strongly recommend a Polyester-filled, hollow-fibre
                          [continental quilt which *(60)*
has a TOG rating of 11.5. The high   *(70)*
TOG rating ensures that you will always be snug and   *(80)*
warm. The quilt is also extremely light in weight because *(90)*
of its Terylene hollow filaments and is hygienically
                                    [enclosed in *(100)*
a hundred per cent cotton cover.
    I attach our latest   *(110)*
price list together with a sample brochure and shall be   *(120)*
pleased to see you at the showrooms when you have   *(130)*
made your choice.
    Yours faithfully.   *(135)*

13 ...⌐... new-style   .... justifiably

.... amateur   .... self-adhesive

.....|V.C.... P.V.C.   .... manipulate

.........↲.... silicone   ....↲... grease

.........↲... waterproof   ....↲.... fadeless

.....↲... in due course   ....↲.... proud

Dear Sirs, Thank you for the interest you have expressed   *(10)*
in our new-style lettering systems.

We are justifiably proud (20)
of our claim that they are so simple to use (30)
that a complete amateur will be able to produce
[professional- (40)
style notices, while having the added attraction of keeping
[costs (50)
down.
As you will see from the enclosed samples, they (60)
are made from self-adhesive P.V.C. material which (70)
is flexible and easy to manipulate. We invite you to (80)
attach them to a clean, dry surface free from silicone (90)
polishes and grease to see for yourself the high standard (100)
which can be attained.
The lettering comes in a range (110)
of colours and sizes in both letters and numbers. It (120)
is fadeless and waterproof and can be used either inside (130)
or out of doors for a really permanent job. We (140)
enclose a catalogue and price list and look forward to (150)
receiving an order from you in due course.
Yours faithfully. (160)

14 ......⌇....... Lockwood ....⌒....... so much

...⌇...... overshadowed .....⌒..... around

...⌒....... worn out ....⌒.... armchair

......⌒.... telephonist

Dear Miss Lockwood,
Although we are still enjoying the holiday (10)
season, it is never too soon to start thinking about (20)
Christmas shopping and I enclose our catalogue with a
[selection (30)
of gifts.
So much of our winter shopping is overshadowed (40)
by the thought of Christmas which makes us spend so (50)
much time rushing around in busy shops that by the (60)
time Christmas is here we are often too worn out (70)
to enjoy it.
While looking through our catalogue you can (80)

relax in your favourite armchair and plan your spending in (90)
your own home without worrying about the crowds or the (100)
weather.

Another advantage is that you can avoid the problem (110)
of paying all your bills at the same time by (120)
buying our goods on four months' free credit. For your (130)
convenience we invite you to make use of our new (140)
telephone ordering service whereby our telephonist can

[tap into the (150)
computer during your call to check whether the goods you (160)
need are available from stock.

With best wishes,

Yours sincerely. (170)

15 .... out of doors .... hearing people

.... lipread .... matter of course

.... lonely people .... hard of hearing

.... hard to understand .... young people

.... middle-aged

Have you ever thought what it would be like to (10)
be deaf? If you have ever had a really bad (20)
cold, you may have experienced a slight deafness for a (30)
short time. It is quite frightening to discover that you (40)
cannot hear in the normal way. We rely far more (50)
on our sense of hearing than we realize, especially out (60)
of doors, where noise often warns us of approaching danger. (70)
People who are deaf are cut off from many pleasures (80)
which hearing people accept as a matter of course. As (90)
it is difficult to hold a conversation with those who (100)
are hard of hearing, unless they are able to lipread, (110)
many deaf people are also very lonely people. This being (120)
so, I find it hard to understand why so many (130)
young people risk deafness by listening to extremely loud

[music, (140)
as research shows that those who work in noisy factories (150)
do, in some degree, become deaf in time. The human (160)

92

ear is a very delicate instrument and once damaged it   *(170)*
cannot be repaired. Many of the young people of today   *(180)*
may be deaf by the time they are middle-aged   *(190)*
if they do not realize the danger of too much   *(200)*
noise and do something about it before it is too   *(210)*
late.   *(211)*

Appendix: Word Groupings List

Some useful groupings for reference

.... able to obtain

.... above all

.... above-mentioned

.... above the

.... Act of Parliament

.... add to the

.... added to the

.... all over the country

.... all over the district

.... all over the world

.... all parts of the world

.... all sorts of things

.... annual return

.... annual review

.... annual turnover

.... application form

.... as soon as

.... as soon as possible

.... at home and abroad

.... at once

.... at the moment

.... at the present time

.... bear in mind

.... before very long

.... best of my ability

.... best of our ability

.... best of their ability

.... best of your ability

.... board of directors

.... Board of Trade

.... borough council

.... business letter

.... by all accounts

.... by all means

.... by means of

.... by no means

...C... can you

...⳽... come/came to the conclusion

...⳽... or ...⳽... capital expenditure

...⳽... capital requirements

...⳽... cash discount

...⳽... cash on delivery

(...⳽... C.O.D.)

...⳽... circulated statement

...⳽... claim for compensation

...∧... day after day

...∧... day after tomorrow

...∧... day before yesterday

...∧... day by day

...⳽... declare a dividend

...𝒈... disc jockey

...∕... during their

...ᴄ... each day

...ɦ... enabled (to)

...𝔁... executive committee

...𝔁ᴄ... export company

...ƒ𝒇... faster and faster

...ɦᴄ... finance committee

...⳽... first and foremost

...⳽... first class

...⳽ɦ... first hand

...⳽ɦ... first-hand information

...⳽ᴄ... first instance

...⳽... first time

...⳽ll... for ever and ever

...⳽ˣ... for example

...⳽ɦ... free of charge

...ᴇᴇ𝒱... further and further

...ᴇ𝒾𝒻... further information

...ᶀᶀ... half-and-half

...ᶀ... half an hour

...𝒱₆... having been

...lᐟⱽ... higher and higher

...ɦ... Hon. Member

...∼... hour after hour

95

.... hour by hour		.... in the meantime
.... Houses of Parliament		.... in the morning
.... I am pleased		.... in the north
.... I am pleased to report		.... in these days
.... I am sorry		.... in those days
.... immediate attention		.... in view (of)
.... in all probability		.... in your company
.... in all respects		.... issued capital of the company
.... in any case		.... it is my pleasure
.... in connection (with)		.... larger and larger
.... in existence		.... large measure
.... in fact		.... last but not least
.... in favour		.... last but by no means least
.... in order (to)		.... last minute
.... in order that		.... last time
.... in our opinion		.... last word
.... in our view		.... Leader of the Opposition
.... I now have pleasure		.... legal action
.... in the absence (of)		.... legal liability
.... in the circumstances		

...... life assurance

...... limited liability

...... longer and longer

...... lower and lower

...... margin of profits

...... Member of Parliament

...... members of the public

...... month after month

...... monthly account

...... more and more

...... more or less

...... Mr and Mrs

...... my account

...... name and address

...... names and addresses

...... near future

...... needless to say

...... next to nothing

...... night after night

...... or ...... no doubt

...... nothing else

...... nothing less

...... not only

...... now and then

...... on behalf (of)

...... or ...... on the other hand

...... on top (of)

...... once a week

...... once upon a time

...... our company

...... out of order

...... out of place

...... out of the question

...... over and above

...... over and done with

...... over and over

...... over and over again

...... over their heads

...../...̄.... parts of the world

.....(........ plenty of time

....|........ point of view

....|........ present day

....|........ present time

.....(//..... quicker and quicker

....../...... rating and valuation

....../....... read and adopted

....../....... referring (to)

........l....... send you

........l....... sending you

....s/s...... shorter and shorter

....s.s...... smaller and smaller

...s.s........ social committee

...s.s....... social security

....s.s....... some form (of)

.... some other

....../....... state of affairs

.....s.y.... summing up

...s....y... sum of money

...s.s.y... sums of money

98

.....y........ thank you for your
enquiry

......y...... thank you for your
letter

......y...... thank you for your
order

.....7........ that there/their

......d...... this company

...d....,... this morning

....d......... this summer

.... time of day

.... time of life

.... time of year

.... time to time

.... to him

.... to them

.... tomorrow night

.... to the committee

........h.... unable to

...u....f.... under separate
cover

.....y........ upside down

......y....... up to date

......⟋ ... value added tax

(.... ⟍ ...... V.A.T.)

......⟍⎯⟍...... vote of thanks

⟍⎯⟋ ...... we are pleased to know

.⟍⟋⎯... we are sending you

......⟍⟍...... we enclose

...⟍⟍⎯...... we have received

...⟍⟍⎯.... we should be pleased

......⟍⟍.... with reference (to)

......⟍⟋...... with reference to your letter

..............⟍⟍ .... with us

..............⟍⟍ .... with you

...⟍⟍⟍... or ...⟍⟍... words a minute

(...⟍⟍⟍.... w.a.m.)

....⟍⟍⟍.... year after year

......⟍⟍...... your account

......⟍⟍...... your attention

...⟍⟍⎯... your order

99